Acting Edition

Manahatta

by Mary Kathryn Nagle

I0741009

SAMUEL FRENCH

Copyright © 2024 by Mary Kathryn Nagle
All Rights Reserved

MANAHATTA is fully protected under the copyright laws of the United States of America, the British Commonwealth, including Canada, and all member countries of the Berne Convention for the Protection of Literary and Artistic Works, the Universal Copyright Convention, and/or the World Trade Organization conforming to the Agreement on Trade Related Aspects of Intellectual Property Rights. All rights, including professional and amateur stage productions, recitation, lecturing, public reading, motion picture, radio broadcasting, television, online/digital production, and the rights of translation into foreign languages are strictly reserved.

ISBN 978-0-573-71125-1

www.concordtheatricals.com
www.concordtheatricals.co.uk

FOR PRODUCTION INQUIRIES

UNITED STATES AND CANADA
info@concordtheatricals.com
1-866-979-0447

UNITED KINGDOM AND EUROPE
licensing@concordtheatricals.co.uk
020-7054-7298

Each title is subject to availability from Concord Theatricals Corp., depending upon country of performance. Please be aware that *MANAHATTA* may not be licensed by Concord Theatricals Corp. in your territory. Professional and amateur producers should contact the nearest Concord Theatricals Corp. office or licensing partner to verify availability.

CAUTION: Professional and amateur producers are hereby warned that *MANAHATTA* is subject to a licensing fee. The purchase, renting, lending or use of this book does not constitute a license to perform this title(s), which license must be obtained from Concord Theatricals Corp. prior to any performance. Performance of this title(s) without a license is a violation of federal law and may subject the producer and/or presenter of such performances to civil penalties. Both amateurs and professionals considering a production are strongly advised to apply to the appropriate agent before starting rehearsals, advertising, or booking a theatre. A licensing fee must be paid whether the title(s) is presented for charity or gain and whether or not admission is charged. Professional/Stock licensing fees are quoted upon application to Concord Theatricals Corp.

This work is published by Samuel French, an imprint of Concord Theatricals Corp.

No one shall make any changes in this title(s) for the purpose of production. No part of this book may be reproduced, stored in a retrieval system, scanned, uploaded, or transmitted in any form, by any means, now known or yet to be invented, including mechanical, electronic, digital, photocopying, recording, videotaping, or otherwise, without the prior written permission of the publisher. No one shall share this title(s), or any part of this title(s), through any social media or file hosting websites.

For all inquiries regarding motion picture, television, online/digital and other media rights, please contact Concord Theatricals Corp.

MUSIC AND THIRD-PARTY MATERIALS USE NOTE

Licensees are solely responsible for obtaining formal written permission from copyright owners to use copyrighted music and/or other copyrighted third-party materials (e.g. artworks, logos) in the performance of this play and are strongly cautioned to do so. If no such permission is obtained by the licensee, then the licensee must use only original music and materials that the licensee owns and controls. Licensees are solely responsible and liable for clearances of all third-party copyrighted materials, including without limitation music, and shall indemnify the copyright owners of the play(s) and their licensing agent, Concord Theatricals Corp., against any costs, expenses, losses and liabilities arising from the use of such copyrighted third-party materials by licensees. For music, please contact the appropriate music licensing authority in your territory for the rights to any incidental music.

IMPORTANT BILLING AND CREDIT REQUIREMENTS

If you have obtained performance rights to this title, please refer to your licensing agreement for important billing and credit requirements.

MANAHATTA was first produced by the Oregon Shakespeare Company (Bill Rauch, Artistic Director; Cynthia Rider, Executive Director) and received its world premiere on March 28th, 2018. The performance was directed by Laurie Woolery, with Scenic Design by Mariana Sánchez, Costume Design by E.B. Brooks, Lighting Design by James F. Ingalls, Projection Design by Mark Holthusen, and Sound Design and Composition by Paul James Prendergast. The Production Stage Manager was Karl Alphonso. The cast was as follows:

LE-LE-WA'-YOU/JANE . . . . Tanis Parenteau

TOOSH-KI-PA-KWIS-I/DEBRA . . . . Rainbow Dickerson

MOTHER/BOBBIE . . . . Sheila Tousey

SE-KET-TU-MAY-QUA/LUKE . . . . Steven Flores

PETER MINUIT/DICK . . . . Jeffrey King

JAKOB/JOE . . . . Danforth Comins

JONAS MICHAELIUS/MICHAEL . . . . David Kelly

MANAHATTA received its East Coast premiere at the Yale Repertory Theatre (James Bundy, Artistic Director; Victoria Nolan, Managing Director) on January 24th, 2020. The performance was directed by Laurie Woolery, with Scenic Design by Mariana Sánchez, Costume Design by Stephanie Bahniuk, Lighting Design by Emma Deane, Hair and Wig Design by Matthew Armentrout, Projection Design by Mark Holthusen, and Sound Design and Composition by Paul James Prendergast. The Production Stage Manager was Julia Bates. The cast was as follows:

LE-LE-WA'-YOU/JANE . . . . Lily Gladstone

TOOSH-KI-PA-KWIS-I/DEBRA . . . . Shyla Lefner

MOTHER/BOBBIE . . . . Carla-Rae

SE-KET-TU-MAY-QUA/LUKE . . . . Steven Flores

PETER MINUIT/DICK . . . . Jeffrey King

JAKOB/JOE . . . . Danforth Comins

JONAS MICHAELIUS/MICHAEL . . . . T. Ryder Smith

MANAHATTA was originally developed by The Public Theater (Oskar Eustis, Artistic Director; Patrick Willingham, Executive Director) and received its Off-Broadway premiere there on November 16th, 2023. The performance was directed by Laurie Woolery, with Scenic Design by Marcelo Martínez García, Costume Design by Lux Haac, Lighting Design by Jeanette Oi-Suk Yew, Hair and Wig Design by Younghawk Bautista, and Sound Design by Paul James Prendergast. The Production Stage Manager was Amanda Nita Luke-Sayed. The cast was as follows:

LE-LE-WA'-YOU/JANE . . . . Elizabeth Frances

TOOSH-KI-PA-KWIS-I/DEBRA. . . . . Rainbow Dickerson

MOTHER/BOBBIE . . . . Sheila Tousey

SE-KET-TU-MAY-QUA/LUKE . . . . Enrico Nassi

PETER MINUIT/DICK . . . . Jeffrey King

JAKOB/JOE. . . . . Joe Tapper

JONAS MICHAELIUS/MICHAEL. . . . . David Kelly

CHARACTERS

LE-LE-WA'-YOU/JANE – (Female, Lenape, late twenties to early thirties.) Le-le-wa'-you is Jane's ancestor living on Manahatta in the early 1600s. Jane is a citizen of the Delaware Nation.

TOOSH-KI-PA-KWIS-I/DEBRA – (Female, Lenape, early to mid-forties.) Toosh-ki-pa-kwis-i is Debra's ancestor living on Manahatta in the early 1600s. Debra is a citizen of the Delaware Nation. She is Jane's older sister.

MOTHER/BOBBIE – (Female, Lenape, late fifties to early sixties.) Mother is Bobbie's ancestor living on Manahatta in the early 1600s. Bobbie is a citizen of the Delaware Nation and mother to Jane and Debra.

SE-KET-TU-MAY-QUA/LUKE – (Male, Lenape, late twenties to early thirties.) Se-ket-tu-may-qua is Luke's ancestor living on Manahatta in the early 1600s. Luke is a citizen of the Delaware Nation. He is Michael's adopted son and close childhood friend of Jane.

PETER MINUIT/DICK – (Male, white, sixties.) Peter Minuit was Director of the Dutch West India Company in the early 1600s on Manahatta. Dick is the head of a large investment bank called Lehman Brothers.

JAKOB/JOE – (Male, white, forties.) Jakob is a trader with the Dutch West India Company on Manahatta in the early 1600s. Joe is Lehman Brothers' CEO.

JONAS MICHAELIUS/MICHAEL – (Male, white, late fifties to early sixties.) Jonas Michaelius is the first priest for the Dutch church on Manahatta in the early 1600s. Michael is a man living in Anadarko, Oklahoma. He runs his local church's choir and works at a local bank. He adopted Luke when Luke was very young.

SETTING AND TIME

Manahatta takes place in two time periods, simultaneously. One half of the play takes place in Manahatta, in both the 17th and 21st centuries. The other half takes place in modern day Anadarko and Chickasha, Oklahoma.

AUTHOR'S NOTES

Casting:

The cast consists of seven actors total. Each actor must play the character as they are outlined above.

The double casting is not optional.

Staging:

It is important that the two worlds begin separately, but immediately commence on a course that ultimately results in a collision.

Transformation from one character to another should take place in the moment and onstage as much as possible, to make clear to the audience that past and present overlap and coexist. Indeed, they are one and the same. The separate locations should not be conceived of as segregated space on stage. Beyond this proscription, anything is possible.

In some instances, a character's exit or entrance is written into the script. Where it is not, anything is possible. Even where it is, they may not need to exit.

A note on the historical accuracy of the piece:

Although *Manahatta* is based on real events that took place, and was written following interviews with Lenape elders whose ancestors lived on Manahatta hundreds of years ago – *Manahatta* is a work of fiction, and the playwright is not to be mistaken for an expert on Lenape history or culture.

For instance, although Se-ket-tu-may-qua is a significant historical Lenape leader, he was not present at the time of the 1626 "land sale" to Peter Minuit and the Dutch. Se-ket-tu-may-qua (Black Beaver) was a legendary leader of the Lenape in the mid-19th century, when the Delaware Nation was removed from their reservation in Texas and placed where they are today, in Anadarko, Oklahoma. Black Beaver later participated in the Medicine Lodge Treaty negotiations of 1867 and acted as a moderator in inter-tribal councils throughout the 1870s. Thus, although he was not present when some of the events of this play took place, the playwright found it appropriate to name the only male Lenape character after this legendary leader since an elder of the Delaware Nation specifically requested that he be named for his great-great grandfather. To the Delaware Lenape today, Black Beaver continues to serve as an example of traits such as intelligence, integrity, and bravery that comprise the character of the Lenape people.

To learn more about the Lenape, their history, and their culture, please visit:

Delaware Nation, in Anadarko, Oklahoma:
http://www.delawarenation.com

Delaware Tribe, in Bartlesville, Oklahoma:
http://www.delawaretribe.org/tribalsite

DEDICATION

This play is dedicated to all Lenape, past and present, but to a few Lenape in particular whose contributions have formed the inspiration for this play: Chris Moore, Paula Pechonick, Joe Baker, Linda Poolaw, Harold Pruner, and Curtis Zunigha. Your survival today is a testament to the strength of your people.

A very special thanks to the Delaware Nation and Delaware Tribe. Without your support, stories, inspiration, and encouragement, this play would never have been possible.

W'anishi

Manahatta is also dedicated to Robert Owens Greygrass. As the very first person to bring Robert Snake to life in the March 27, 2013 reading at the Public Theater, we will always remember Robert with deep gratitude for all that he did to share not only this story, but all Native stories.

This play would not have been possible without the support and guidance I received from the Lenape Center, especially their co-founders, Joe Baker and Curtis Zunigha. Also, many thanks to Se-ket-tu-may-qua's great-grandson Harold Pruner, who encouraged me to fashion a character after and in honor of his grandfather. Manahatta is, always has been, and will continue to be a sacred home.

One

(Manhattan. Summer 2002.)

*(**JOE** sits behind his desk in his office. **JANE** enters.)*

JOE. You're late.

JANE. I was lost.

JOE. Lost?

JANE. I got on the subway going the wrong way.

JOE. I never ride the subway.

JANE. You live close enough to walk.

JOE. I take my helicopter.

JANE. Oh.

JOE. You can sit down. That's what the chair's for.

*(**JANE** sits.)*

So you want to work at an investment bank.

JANE. Yes.

JOE. But not a commercial bank?

JANE. Commercial bankers make loans.

JOE. What's wrong with that?

JANE. I want to underwrite securities. You know, work with stocks and bonds –

JOE. Because you think that's sexy?

JANE. I think it's challenging.

JOE. You want to be challenged?

JANE. Yes.

JOE. Go to law school.

JANE. I don't like to argue –

JOE. You're arguing now.

JANE. I'm not arguing, I'm explaining –

JOE. So be a teacher.

JANE. That sounds boring.

JOE. *(Looking at her résumé.)* You studied math. At MIT. That sounds boring.

JANE. What do you know about math?

JOE. Enough to know I don't want to talk about it.

JANE. I got my degree in Financial Mathematics –

JOE. I'm asleep already.

JANE. Math is very important.

JOE. So is brushing your teeth. But we aren't gonna pay you to do it. Look, number one in your class at MIT, Stanford business school. I get it. You're smart. But we interview a lot of people that are smart for this position. Most of them don't want it. Like you, they graduate from some fancy schmancy Ivy League school at the top of their class, but they have no idea what they want to do with their lives. They see this as a place where they can go and make money. Lots of it. But at the end of the day, loving money isn't enough. Everyone loves money. To succeed at this job, you need something else. Something more. Do you understand what I'm saying?

JANE. Yes.

JOE. I need to know if you really want this.

> (**JANE** *smiles.*)

Well, that's one less person I need to consider.

JANE. I left my dad. To come here. He's in Oklahoma, and I'm here –

JOE. Dads generally don't participate in our interviews.

JANE. He's in the hospital, having open heart surgery.

JOE. You mean...like right now?

JANE. Your secretary said you wouldn't reschedule –

JOE. Ordinarily no, but for something like this –

JANE. I want this job. That's why I'm here. I know the other candidates, the others you've interviewed. I went to school with them. I competed against them. But I am not one of them. I didn't go to Stanford because my parents told me to. My parents didn't graduate from high school. I went to Stanford because I knocked down every obstacle they placed in my way.

> (**JOE** *signs a piece of paper and hands it to* **JANE**.*)*

What's this?

JOE. Your paperwork. Take this to my secretary. She'll introduce you to your managing director –

JANE. Does this mean –

JOE. I'm assigning you to the RMBS Group –

JANE. Did you just hire me?!

JOE. Ms. Snake, you work on Wall Street now. If you let others see you get this excited about success, you'll never have more of it.

> (**JANE** *nods.*)

JOE. And let me tell you something about Manhattan. When you're not from here, when you're from somewhere else, this place can be hell. It'll eat you up, chew you up, and spit you out. There will be days when you think everyone is against you.

But if you stick it out, if you give it all you got, you'll see, Manhattan has more to offer than any other place in the world.

Two

(Anadarko, Oklahoma. Three days later.)

*(**BOBBIE** at the table in her house. She waves a postcard in her hand to ward off the bands of sweat running down her face and neck.)*

BOBBIE. I was hopin' you'd come back with photos. Not postcards. Never asked for postcards of all this crazy stuff. The Umpire State Building. Or what is this –

(Squints as she tries to read from the postcard.)

the Mama Museum? No. Not for me. All I wanted was a photo. Of Manahatta.

JANE. It was a short visit.

BOBBIE. But ya got to see it.

JANE. I did.

BOBBIE. And?

JANE. And then I got on a plane and –

BOBBIE. Yer dad wanted to visit.

JANE. I can't find your necklace.

BOBBIE. I promised him we'd go –

JANE. Mom –

BOBBIE. He wanted to see Pearl Street.

JANE. We're late.

BOBBIE. They named it Pearl Street after the huge mounds of shells we left there along the shore.

JANE. I can't find your wampum.

BOBBIE. Pearl Street is where we got our wampum.

JANE. We need to leave for the church –

BOBBIE. Yer ancestors in Manahatta didn't say goodbye to their relations in a church.

JANE. We're in Oklahoma, not Manahatta.

BOBBIE. When my parents died, we buried them the Indian way.

JANE. Did you take it off in the kitchen?

BOBBIE. When I was a kid, our funerals useta be four days, not four minutes.

JANE. Mom!

BOBBIE. My sock drawer.

*(Exasperated, **JANE** exits to retrieve the necklace from the sock drawer. **DEBRA** enters.)*

DEBRA. You ready to go?

BOBBIE. Almost.

DEBRA. Almost? Everyone is at the church waiting on us and – where's your wampum?

BOBBIE. Janie's lookin' for it.

DEBRA. You wore it, last night –

*(**JANE** enters, carrying the wampum necklace.)*

JANE. Found it.

*(**BOBBIE** stands up to put on the necklace. She struggles to clasp it behind her neck.)*

DEBRA. I knew this would happen.

JANE. I couldn't find the necklace.

DEBRA. I told you that if I left to take the food you would have to get Mom ready.

JANE. It's not my fault things are disorganized around here.

BOBBIE. I told you, the sock drawer –

DEBRA. It's been sitting in the same sock drawer for thirty-five years.

JANE. Sorry, that's the last place I thought to look.

DEBRA. I guess they don't teach you to use common sense in grad school.

BOBBIE. Someone help me with this.

DEBRA. Give it to me.

BOBBIE. Why the heck we gotta do this in a church anyways?

DEBRA. That's what Dad wanted.

BOBBIE. He never told me that.

DEBRA. Maybe you never listened.

BOBBIE. You tryin' to choke me?

DEBRA. Hold still.

(**DEBRA** *continues working on the necklace around* **BOBBIE***'s neck.*)

BOBBIE. *(To* **DEBRA***.)* She got the job, ya know.

DEBRA. We're late.

BOBBIE. She's gonna live in Manahatta.

DEBRA. Whole church's waitin' on us.

BOBBIE. What exactly ya gonna do?

JANE. It's complicated.

BOBBIE. Better be. Had to go to school ten years to do it.

JANE. I'll be working at an investment bank.

DEBRA. They let Indians do that?

JANE. Yes, Debra, they do.

DEBRA. I bet you're the only Indian.

> **(SE-KET-TU-MAY-QUA** *enters, carrying furs for scraping.)*

JANE. I might be.

DEBRA. I'd hate to live in Manhattan.

JANE. Good thing you don't have to.

DEBRA. It's all concrete and skyscrapers and there's no leaves, no trees, no sky –

JANE. There's sky in Manhattan –

DEBRA. No grass –

JANE. You've never been there –

DEBRA. I've seen pictures.

JANE. *(To* **DEBRA.***)* You have no idea what you're talking about.

BOBBIE. None a ya do.

> **(SE-KET-TU-MAY-QUA** *places a fur in front of* **JANE.***)*

That's the problem with your generation. Ya got no idea where you came from.

Three

(17th-century Manahatta. Autumn.)

SE-KET-TU-MAY-QUA. We have to scrape harder.

(BOBBIE *and* **DEBRA** *exit.)*

The pieces at the end are the hardest.

LE-LE-WA'-YOU. Have you ever worn a fur without the fat?

SE-KET-TU-MAY-QUA. Of course not.

LE-LE-WA'-YOU. There's a reason the Creator gave the beaver his fat. It protects our skin.

SE-KET-TU-MAY-QUA. Of course.

LE-LE-WA'-YOU. So why are we scraping it away?

SE-KET-TU-MAY-QUA. White women don't want the fat.

LE-LE-WA'-YOU. How do they protect their skin?

SE-KET-TU-MAY-QUA. White women don't live in the beaver like you and I do. They only wear it for...special occasions.

LE-LE-WA'-YOU. Like when they give birth?

SE-KET-TU-MAY-QUA. No. Like...when they walk down a street.

LE-LE-WA'-YOU. Oh.

SE-KET-TU-MAY-QUA. Or when they visit someone. You know, to eat.

LE-LE-WA'-YOU. Eat what?

SE-KET-TU-MAY-QUA. Something special.

> *(***LE-LE-WA'-YOU*** considers this. She places the fur on her shoulders, imitating what she imagines to be a white woman in a beaver fur.)*

LE-LE-WA'-YOU. Hello. Do you see my fur?

SE-KET-TU-MAY-QUA. I do.

LE-LE-WA'-YOU. I put it on so that we could have a special occasion.

SE-KET-TU-MAY-QUA. I'm so glad that you did.

LE-LE-WA'-YOU. Would you like to walk down a street?

SE-KET-TU-MAY-QUA. With you, I'd walk anywhere.

(Beat.)

LE-LE-WA'-YOU. So you've seen them?

SE-KET-TU-MAY-QUA. The traders?

LE-LE-WA'-YOU. The women, wearing our furs.

SE-KET-TU-MAY-QUA. Oh, no. The Dutch didn't bring women. They only brought men.

LE-LE-WA'-YOU. They left their women behind?

SE-KET-TU-MAY-QUA. I guess so.

LE-LE-WA'-YOU. Why?

SE-KET-TU-MAY-QUA. I don't know. I just trade with the men. And then they load our furs on giant boats and take them to their women, across the water.

LE-LE-WA'-YOU. You must see a lot at the market.

SE-KET-TU-MAY-QUA. I do.

LE-LE-WA'-YOU. Next time you go, I'll come with you.

SE-KET-TU-MAY-QUA. No.

LE-LE-WA'-YOU. No?

SE-KET-TU-MAY-QUA. It's dangerous.

LE-LE-WA'-YOU. I've traded for years. Up and down the Broad Way.

SE-KET-TU-MAY-QUA. With other Tribal Nations. This is different.

LE-LE-WA'-YOU. And that makes it dangerous?

SE-KET-TU-MAY-QUA. They don't trade the same way we do.

LE-LE-WA'-YOU. What is that supposed to mean?

SE-KET-TU-MAY-QUA. I've seen them do things…things I have to believe are only possible if you leave your women behind.

(**MICHAEL** *enters, carrying a casserole.*)

MICHAEL. Jane! Thought we might see you here.

(**MICHAEL** *hands the casserole to* **SE-KET-TU-MAY-QUA**.*)*

Four

(Anadarko, Oklahoma. The next day. Outside of Bobbie's house.)

JANE. Michael. Luke. Good to see you.

MICHAEL. Funeral sure was beautiful. What were there, three hundred? Four hundred people there? We ran out of chairs, had to ask folks to stand. Outside. Never seen that many folks at a service.

JANE. I'm on my way to the store.

MICHAEL. Well now, don't let us stop you. We just came by to pay our respects.

*(**JANE** looks at **LUKE**. **LUKE** looks at **MICHAEL**. **MICHAEL** takes the casserole from **LUKE**.)*

I'll check on Bobbie.

*(**MICHAEL** exits.)*

JANE. Thanks for coming.

LUKE. Of course.

JANE. Sorry we didn't get a chance to talk.

LUKE. There were a lot of people there.

(Beat.)

Hey, how you like working in Manhattan?

JANE. I haven't started yet.

LUKE. Oh, I thought –

JANE. I was interviewing. The morning Dad passed. That's when I got the job.

LUKE. Oh.

JANE. Yeah.

LUKE. How could you know? No one thought that, I saw him the day before, and he told me it would be a routine procedure.

JANE. No one remembers the conversations we had before his surgery. They just remember I wasn't there.

(Beat.)

LUKE. Manhattan. I always knew you'd end up somewhere like that.

I knew that in third grade. You came in on the second day of school and you'd already memorized all of the multiplication tables. In one night.

JANE. I helped you –

LUKE. You sure did.

JANE. I taught you tricks. That's all it is. Games and tricks. To remember things.

LUKE. Your birthday is the fourteenth –

JANE. Yours is the seventh –

LUKE. Of February.

JANE. And that's a two. So two times seven –

LUKE & JANE. Makes fourteen.

(Beat.)

JANE. Come visit me.

LUKE. Can you picture me in Manhattan?

JANE. As a matter of fact, I can.

LUKE. It's so fancy.

JANE. Not really –

LUKE. Everyone wears a suit –

JANE. And rides on subways full of trash and graffiti –

LUKE. Even in a suit, I look out of place.

JANE. How do you think I feel when I come back? Everyone just stares at me.

LUKE. It's hard not to.

> *(Beat.)*

He always talked about you, at church. He was so proud. Jane's doing this. Jane's doing that. Even on Easter Sunday, you were all he could talk about.

> *(**MICHAEL** knocks on Bobbie's door. **BOBBIE** attempts to shove the bills to the side of the table.)*

BOBBIE. Come in.

> *(**MICHAEL** knocks again.)*

Come in or go away. Those are your options.

> *(**MICHAEL** knocks again.)*

Jesus.

> *(**BOBBIE** answers the door.)*

Michael.

> *(**JANE** exits.)*

MICHAEL. Hope I'm not intruding.

BOBBIE. No, not at all.

MICHAEL. How you doin'?

BOBBIE. I'm doin' just fine. So there. We've covered that subject. Now we don't gotta talk 'bout it. Come on in.

MICHAEL. I can just drop this off and then –

BOBBIE. I'll get you some coffee.

MICHAEL. Oh, no thanks. I don't drink coffee.

BOBBIE. You don't drink coffee?

MICHAEL. I prefer tea.

BOBBIE. Well ain't got no tea 'round here. Ya know us Indians, we can't drink tea.

MICHAEL. I didn't know that.

BOBBIE. If we drink too much tea, we drown in our own tea pee.

(**MICHAEL** *is unsure how to react.*)

It's a joke.

MICHAEL. That's a good one.

(**LUKE** *enters the home.*)

BOBBIE. Where were you?

LUKE. Talking to Jane.

BOBBIE. She went shopping. For vegetables. What'd you bring us?

LUKE. Shepherd's pie.

MICHAEL. My wife made it.

BOBBIE. Looks like a casserole to me.

MICHAEL. It is –

BOBBIE. *(To* **LUKE**.*)* Got frybread?

LUKE. Uh, no.

BOBBIE. You came to visit me without frybread?

MICHAEL. My wife doesn't know how to make frybread.

BOBBIE. Your son does. I taught him.

(To **LUKE**.*)* Come by anytime, I'll always make ya frybread.

MICHAEL. Your husband meant a lot to me, personally, and to our whole church.

BOBBIE. He loved singing in your choir.

MICHAEL. He was the best we had. Not sure how we're gonna replace him.

(*Beat.*)

Well, I just wanted to stop by and pay my respects.

BOBBIE. Thanks for the pie.

MICHAEL. We'd love to see you in church.

BOBBIE. You did. Yesterday.

MICHAEL. You know, on a more regular basis.

BOBBIE. Don't hold your breath.

(**MICHAEL** *goes to place the shepherd's pie down on the table.* **BOBBIE** *intercepts.*)

I'll take that.

(*She places the casserole next to the bills.*)

MICHAEL. Well now, we'll be on our way.

(**MICHAEL** *gestures to* **LUKE** *and they turn to go.*)

BOBBIE. I heard your commercial.

(**MICHAEL** *stops. He turns to her.*)

For the bank. You must be busy, I imagine.

MICHAEL. Business is good.

(**BOBBIE** *picks up a bill and hands it to* **MICHAEL**. **MICHAEL** *looks at it. His eyes widen.*)

BOBBIE. IHS wouldn't, they wouldn't pay for the surgery. When that heart doctor in the city told us Charlie needed surgery, Charlie, he didn't want it. Not if it meant his girls would have to pay for it. He knew he couldn't afford it. So I promised him, I told him I'd cover the whole thing. Even if it meant I had to work 'til the day I die.

(*Beat.*)

How does a surgery cost sixty thousand?

(**MICHAEL** *puts his arm around* **BOBBIE**.)

The girls don't know.

MICHAEL. We won't tell them. Right Luke?

BOBBIE. You can't tell them.

LUKE. I won't.

BOBBIE. Deb will be back any minute –

MICHAEL. The church, we got programs, you know for folks that –

BOBBIE. Don't need the church's handouts, I just gotta work. 'Til I get it paid off.

(*Beat.*)

Your bank, you let people borrow money.

MICHAEL. Are you talking about a loan?

BOBBIE. Yes. Yes, that's it.

MICHAEL. For a loan, you would need collateral.

BOBBIE. Oh. I see. Foolish, I know. But I ain't never had a loan, don't got no credit cards –

MICHAEL. No credit score. I get it. At the bank, we've got loans for folks like you, with no credit score. But we would need an asset. Perhaps your house.

(*Beat.*)

MICHAEL. Of course, there's always bankruptcy.

BOBBIE. Bankruptcy?

MICHAEL. If you're worried about using your home –

BOBBIE. No. This is my debt. I promised him I'd pay these bills. I never break a promise.

>   *(Beat.)*

MICHAEL. You know, Luke works with me now.

BOBBIE. At the bank?

LUKE. They make me wear a suit.

MICHAEL. Small potatoes compared to what Jane'll be doing in Manhattan, I'm sure.

BOBBIE. Ya gotta start somewhere.

>   *(Beat.)*

MICHAEL. Well. Luke and I, we could come back sometime with paperwork. For a loan application.

BOBBIE. I'd like that.

MICHAEL. Alright then.

BOBBIE. *(To **LUKE**.)* Hey. Next time you visit me, I expect frybread.

>   *(**LUKE** smiles. **LUKE** and **MICHAEL** exit.
>   **BOBBIE** watches them go. She picks up the
>   bills and shoves them into the drawer.)*

Five

(Anadarko, the Front Porch of Bobbie's home. Two days later.)

*(**DEBRA** sits on the porch singing a Lenape hymn.)*

DEBRA. *(Singing.)*
NO-WA-TONE, NO-WA-TONE,
HAY-LAY-LOIEMA, GEE-SHAY-LOIEMA.
NO-WA-TONE, NO-WA-TONE,
HAY-LAY-LOIEMA, GEE-SHAY-LOIEMA.

*(**DEBRA** stops when she sees **JANE**.)*

Mom asked me to move in with her.

JANE. Oh.

DEBRA. She doesn't want to be alone. She asked me 'cause she can't ask you. I mean, she could ask you, but the answer would be no. We all know you're never moving back.

(Beat.)

You ready for your first day? On Wall Street?

JANE. I'm sorta terrified.

DEBRA. You'll do great.

JANE. Was that the song you put in the ANA proposal?

DEBRA. It was.

JANE. Sounded like a prayer.

DEBRA. It's a hymn.

JANE. In Delaware?

DEBRA. "God I know you love me." Daddy always said, you don't know a language until you can sing it and pray it.

JANE. He was so excited when you agreed to help him submit the application for the language program.

You sent it in April, right?

(**DEBRA** *nods.*)

When do you think you'll hear back?

(*Beat.*)

Deb?

DEBRA. We didn't get it.

JANE. What? When did you find out?

DEBRA. Last week.

JANE. You didn't tell me.

DEBRA. So much was going on.

JANE. Did you tell Dad?

DEBRA. Are you kidding me? He woulda died right then and there.

JANE. Can you apply again next year?

DEBRA. Yeah. We can apply every year for the next fifty years. Doesn't mean we'll get it.

JANE. You'll get it. I know you will.

DEBRA. It's really competitive. All the tribes applying for one small pool of money. Turns out everyone needs a language program.

(*Beat.*)

Just before he passed, he said Debra, when you get that grant, ask yer mom to teach.

JANE. Mom? She's never said a word in Lenape.

DEBRA. Daddy said when they first met, it was all she spoke.

(Beat.)

JANE. You said the surgery would fix the blockage.

DEBRA. That's what the doctor said.

JANE. I didn't think it would happen so fast.

DEBRA. No one did.

JANE. You didn't call me.

DEBRA. There was a lot going on –

JANE. I didn't get to say goodbye.

DEBRA. You want everyone to think the most important thing in your life is family – but you and I both know that's a lie. You left, Jane. A long time ago. And no one, not even Daddy, could convince you to come home.

*(**JAKOB** enters and approaches **JANE**.)*

JAKOB. Well hello there.

Six

(Manahatta. **JAKOB** *speaks to* **LE-LE-WA'-YOU,**
who has come to the market to trade furs.)

JAKOB. I don't believe I've seen you before. At the market.
If you don't mind my asking, what are you doing here?

*(***DEBRA*** *exits.)*

LE-LE-WA'-YOU. <u>Nkata ashuntesu</u> (I want to trade.)

> *(***LE-LE-WA'-YOU*** *proudly displays her
> beautiful furs that she has brought to
> market.)*

JAKOB. Your fur is very beautiful.

> *(***LE-LE-WA'-YOU*** *extends her fur, wanting to
> make a trade.)*

LE-LE-WA'-YOU. <u>Telen ok naxa</u> (Thirteen.)

JAKOB. I'm afraid I don't understand.

LE-LE-WA'-YOU. <u>Telen ok naxa</u> (Thirteen.)

JAKOB. I don't know what you're saying –

LE-LE-WA'-YOU. <u>Keku hach katatam</u> (What do you want)?

JAKOB. But I would be very happy to trade with you.

> *(***SE-KET-TU-MAY-QUA*** *enters.)*

SE-KET-TU-MAY-QUA. <u>Awen hech nan</u> (Who is that person?)

LE-LE-WA'-YOU. <u>Ashuntesu</u> (He trades.)

SE-KET-TU-MAY-QUA. <u>Ki chi hach ne le</u> (Is that really so?)

LE-LE-WA'-YOU. <u>Ahi kta</u> (Yes.)

SE-KET-TU-MAY-QUA. *(Gestures to the fur in her arms.)*
<u>Kexa hech</u> (How much?)

LE-LE-WA'-YOU. <u>Taktani</u> (I don't know.)

JAKOB. I'm awfully sorry if I've caused some sort of problem here –

SE-KET-TU-MAY-QUA. No problem. No problem at all. How much?

JAKOB. What?

SE-KET-TU-MAY-QUA. How much will you pay for her fur?

JAKOB. You can speak.

SE-KET-TU-MAY-QUA. So can you, it seems.

JAKOB. I've only ever met two Indians who can speak.

SE-KET-TU-MAY-QUA. Now you've met three. How much will you pay?

JAKOB. I've brought wampum.

SE-KET-TU-MAY-QUA. One fathom.

JAKOB. I'll pay a quarter.

SE-KET-TU-MAY-QUA. Three quarters.

JAKOB. That's more than I usually pay for three furs.

SE-KET-TU-MAY-QUA. This is the finest quality you'll find on the island. Le-le-wa'-you scraped it all by herself.

JAKOB. *(To* **LE-LE-WA'-YOU**.*)* Le-le-wa'-you? That's your name?

> (**LE-LE-WA'-YOU** *nods in recognition of her name.)*

LE-LE-WA'-YOU. <u>Keku hech kteluwensi</u> (What is your name?)

> (**JAKOB** *isn't sure how to respond.)*

SE-KET-TU-MAY-QUA. She'd like to know your name.

JAKOB. Oh.

(*Points to himself.*) Jakob.

(*She smiles.*)

LE-LE-WA'-YOU. Jakob. <u>Weli kishku</u> (It is a good day.)

JAKOB. Here's one fathom.

(**JAKOB** *hands over one fathom.*)

SE-KET-TU-MAY-QUA. (*To* **LE-LE-WA'-YOU.**) <u>Kweti</u> (One) fathom.

LE-LE-WA'-YOU. <u>Echei</u> (Oh my gosh!)

(**LE-LE-WA'-YOU** *hands* **JAKOB** *her furs.*)

SE-KET-TU-MAY-QUA. (*To* **JAKOB.**) If you even try to touch her –

JAKOB. We were trading.

SE-KET-TU-MAY-QUA. I've seen what your men do to our women.

JAKOB. I would never do that.

SE-KET-TU-MAY-QUA. So you're the exception.

JAKOB. I promise you. I trade with the best intentions.

(**JAKOB** *exits.*)

LE-LE-WA'-YOU. What'd you say to him?

SE-KET-TU-MAY-QUA. What are you doing here?

LE-LE-WA'-YOU. Trading. Just like you.

SE-KET-TU-MAY-QUA. You have no idea what you're doing.

LE-LE-WA'-YOU. It's really quite simple. I give him fur, he gives me wampum.

SE-KET-TU-MAY-QUA. He may be fine. It's the others I worry about.

LE-LE-WA'-YOU. I don't need you to protect me.

SE-KET-TU-MAY-QUA. You can't even speak their language.

LE-LE-WA'-YOU. *(Bold and demanding, without a hint of vulnerability or servitude.)* So teach me.

(*Beat.*)

If you won't, I'll find someone who will. One of them maybe.

SE-KET-TU-MAY-QUA. It's not that simple.

LE-LE-WA'-YOU. If you can learn their language, why can't I?

(*Beat.*)

SE-KET-TU-MAY-QUA. <u>Keku hech katatam</u> (What do you want?)

(Slow and instructive.) What do you want?

LE-LE-WA'-YOU. *(Struggles to pronounce the words.)* What do you want?

SE-KET-TU-MAY-QUA. *(Slow and instructive.)* What do you want?

LE-LE-WA'-YOU. What do you want?

SE-KET-TU-MAY-QUA. *(Asks as a question in the lesson.)* What do you want?

LE-LE-WA'-YOU. *(Responds.)* <u>Nkata utenink a</u> (I want to go to town.)

(**SE-KET-TU-MAY-QUA** *smiles in response.*)

SE-KET-TU-MAY-QUA. <u>Keku hech likte</u> (What color is it?)

(Slow and instructive.) What color is it?

LE-LE-WA'-YOU. *(Works hard to repeat the strange new sounds.)* What color is it?

SE-KET-TU-MAY-QUA. What color is it?

LE-LE-WA'-YOU. *(Points to fur.)* <u>Se ke</u> (Black.)

SE-KET-TU-MAY-QUA. Black.

LE-LE-WA'-YOU. Black.

SE-KET-TU-MAY-QUA. Very good!

(Slow and instructive.) You know it!

      (**LE-LE-WA'-YOU** *does not understand.*)

<u>Kuwatun</u> (You know it.)

(Slow and instructive.) You know it.

      (**LE-LE-WA'-YOU** *nods with understanding.*)

LE-LE-WA'-YOU. <u>W'anishi</u> (Thank you.)

SE-KET-TU-MAY-QUA. *(Slow and instructive.)* I love you.

LE-LE-WA'-YOU. ?

SE-KET-TU-MAY-QUA. <u>Ktaholel</u> (I love you.)

      (**LE-LE-WA'-YOU** *is taken aback.*)

(Slow and instructive.) I love you.

LE-LE-WA'-YOU. <u>Ktaholel</u> (I love you.)

      (A kiss.)

Seven

(Manahatta. Autumn.)

*(**PETER MINUIT** sits behind his desk. **JAKOB** enters, clutching two furs. He presents the furs to **PETER MINUIT**. **PETER MINUIT** stares at the furs.)*

JAKOB. Two, sir.

PETER MINUIT. *(Gestures to the tulip on his desk.)* How much do you think I paid for this tulip?

JAKOB. Five hundred.

PETER MINUIT. No.

JAKOB. Six hundred.

PETER MINUIT. Twelve hundred guilders. When I bought this beauty, she was the most expensive tulip. In the world.

JAKOB. She's beautiful.

PETER MINUIT. Of course now the Company's wealthiest investors are paying sixteen hundred, eighteen hundred, sometimes two thousand guilders, for a tulip. I promise you, their tulips are no different than mine. The tulips aren't changing. Only the price the market is willing to pay for them. Close your eyes. I said close your eyes.

(Checks to make sure they're closed.)

Now picture Manahatta. The southern tip, full of boats. From all over the world. Sweden. Britain. Russia. France – they've all come here to trade.

JAKOB. Tulips?

PETER MINUIT. No, you idiot. Furs. Because we have the finest furs in the New World. Scraped by savage hands. And people want to buy them. But we can only sell what we have. And right now we have very little. Like two. Which is far from enough.

(**JONAS MICHAELIUS** *enters.*)

JONAS MICHAELIUS. Hello.

(*Sees* **JAKOB**.)

My apologies.

PETER MINUIT. Can I help you?

JONAS MICHAELIUS. I'm looking for Peter Minuit, Director of the Dutch West India Company.

PETER MINUIT. You found him.

JONAS MICHAELIUS. Oh, wonderful.

PETER MINUIT. (*To* **JAKOB**.) You need to trade more.

JAKOB. How much more?

PETER MINUIT. I'm sorry?

JAKOB. How much more is enough?

PETER MINUIT. There's no such thing as enough in the New World.

(*To* **JONAS MICHAELIUS**.) You're Jonas.

JONAS MICHAELIUS. Jonas Michaelius. The Company sent me here to organize the first congregation.

PETER MINUIT. So they tell me. They want us to send them our furs and our prayers.

JONAS MICHAELIUS. We send our prayers to the Lord above, not to any group of people here on Earth.

PETER MINUIT. It was a joke, Jonas.

JONAS MICHAELIUS. Oh, I see.

PETER MINUIT. *(To* **JAKOB.***)* You're excused.

(**JAKOB** *exits.*)

JONAS MICHAELIUS. It's a miracle I even made it here. The boat ride was wretched. My family, we left Amsterdam on the twenty-fourth of January. We were supposed to reach Manahatta by the first of March. But we encountered a tempest in the Bahamas and were trapped on that god-forsaken boat for seventy-five days.

We ran out of food, there was no fresh water, and my wife, I'm surprised she made it. Now she's very, very sick.

PETER MINUIT. The Company let you bring her.

JONAS MICHAELIUS. She's my wife.

PETER MINUIT. The rest of us had to come alone.

JONAS MICHAELIUS. We've been married thirty years.

PETER MINUIT. That's precious. But your marriage may not last –

JONAS MICHAELIUS. We survived the trip. I'm confident we can survive the island.

PETER MINUIT. You'll see for yourself. The women here. They're awfully tempting.

JONAS MICHAELIUS. I've come to share the Gospel.

PETER MINUIT. With the Indians?

JONAS MICHAELIUS. The Company has asked me to.

(**LE-LE-WA'-YOU** *enters, furs in hand.*)

PETER MINUIT. I wish you the best in your endeavors, I truly do. But very few of them speak, and the ones that do have no grasp of basic concepts like capital, commerce, *ownership.* They have no idea how an economy actually works.

JONAS MICHAELIUS. Understanding how an economy functions is one thing. I leave that to you. But hearing and receiving the Lord's word is for all of his children, savage may they be.

(**TOOSH-KI-PA-KWIS-I** *enters.*)

TOOSH-KI-PA-KWIS-I. There you are. It's finally stopped raining and we need to plant the corn. Mother asked me to find you.

Eight

(Manahatta. Spring. **LE-LE-WA'-YOU** *is scraping furs when* **TOOSH-KI-PA-KWIS-I** *approaches.)*

LE-LE-WA'-YOU. Tell her I'm happy to help tomorrow.

TOOSH-KI-PA-KWIS-I. Tomorrow? It might rain tomorrow –

LE-LE-WA'-YOU. I know. That's why I have to scrape today.

TOOSH-KI-PA-KWIS-I. Scrape what?

LE-LE-WA'-YOU. *(Gestures to her pile.)* The furs. White women won't wear them if we don't scrape them.

*(***TOOSH-KI-PA-KWIS-I*** isn't sure what she thinks of that information.)*

And if I really focus, I can trade four or five furs in one day.

TOOSH-KI-PA-KWIS-I. That's a lot of furs.

LE-LE-WA'-YOU. It's a lot of wampum. Just yesterday I brought home four fathoms. For five furs.

TOOSH-KI-PA-KWIS-I. What will you do with all of that wampum?

LE-LE-WA'-YOU. Trade with it.

TOOSH-KI-PA-KWIS-I. For what?

LE-LE-WA'-YOU. More.

TOOSH-KI-PA-KWIS-I. We trade with, not for wampum.

*(***JOE*** enters and approaches **LE-LE-WA'-YOU**.)*

JOE. Your numbers are low.

Nine

(Manhattan. Months later.)

*(***JANE*** *is in Joe's office in Manhattan.)*

JOE. Too low.

*(***TOOSH-KI-PA-KWIS-I*** *exits.)*

JANE. Have you seen my sellers? They never give me the full loan tape on time.

JOE. I'm sure you're frustrated –

JANE. My transaction managers are scrambling to clear loans at the last minute, and I've got sellers like American Dream and ABC trying to jam in prior drops, and I mean, drops like a stated loan with CLTV above ninety.

JOE. You need to close your deals on time.

JANE. I'm just not sure what they're stuffing in these things. So I did some math –

JOE. We didn't hire you to do math.

JANE. If the rate of defaults on home mortgage loans goes above seven percent –

JOE. Which has never happened in the history of the United States.

JANE. But if it does –

JOE. It never will.

JANE. We don't know who's on the other end of these loans. And some of these sellers, they're stuffing in loans with stated income, NO documentation, or twenty thousand a year income on a six hundred K home. Give 'em a few years, but when enough of them default, the securities we sell will be worthless.

JOE. Everything we sell is rated Triple A by S&P and Moody's.

JANE. That's what I don't understand. When I look at the loan tape –

JOE. We didn't hire you to look at the goddamn loan tape, Jesus Snake. I agree, your sellers are the worst, they've definitely gone off the reservation, but you've got to figure out a way to close your deals on time.

JANE. Off the reservation?

JOE. I'm agreeing with you. They're crazy, they don't follow the rules, and let's face it, they're demented. You know, fucked in the head.

JANE. And that means they're off the reservation?

JOE. Oh God, I forgot, you were born on a reservation.

JANE. Actually, I wasn't.

JOE. But you're Native American?

JANE. The federal government took away our reservation and never gave it back.

JOE. Oh. Well, it's just a saying. You know I didn't mean any offense by it. But I am serious about your performance. I like you Snake. And I've been here long enough to see what happens to our Senior Transaction Managers when they don't close deals on time. I don't want to see that happen to you. So get your act together. Don't wanna have to send you back to Oklahoma.

Ten

(Anadarko. A few weeks later.)

*(**MICHAEL** and **LUKE** sit with **BOBBIE** at her kitchen table, surrounded by papers.)*

MICHAEL. OK so your DTI?

BOBBIE. DTI?

MICHAEL. It's a ratio.

BOBBIE. Of what?

LUKE. Debt to income. To apply for a loan you have to tell the bank how much debt you have in comparison to your income.

BOBBIE. That's easy. I got a lot of debt. Hardly no income.

LUKE. You said you have no FICO?

BOBBIE. What's that?

LUKE. Your credit score.

BOBBIE. You said yer bank has a special type a loan, for folks that ain't got no credit score.

MICHAEL. You'll have to get an ARM.

BOBBIE. I got two.

LUKE. Adjustable rate mortgage, it's a product we offer.

MICHAEL. With an ARM, the payments will eventually go up, but it will give you the lowest monthly payments up front. Right now.

BOBBIE. Sign me up.

MICHAEL. Now, one last question. Do you own this house?

BOBBIE. I live here, yeah.

MICHAEL. But do you own it?

BOBBIE. It's my home.

MICHAEL. Is your name on the deed?

BOBBIE. It's on all the bills that come here.

MICHAEL. Look, let's not overly complicate things. In order to take out a loan on this house, we have to show the bank that you own it.

BOBBIE. Grandpa got this land in the Allotment. Built the whole house himself. Didn't get help from nobody. Grandpa and Grandma moved in, and six weeks later, Mom was born. I was born here, then I married Charlie, and he moved in. We had Debra, and seven years later, Creator blessed us with Janie. So for as long as I can remember, this house, for my family, this has been our home.

MICHAEL. I'll ask Debra.

BOBBIE. I told you not to tell her.

MICHAEL. We need to know –

BOBBIE. I need to know you won't tell her. Or Jane.

MICHAEL. I promise.

> (**BOBBIE** *looks to* **LUKE.**)

LUKE. I promise.

BOBBIE. When do I get my money?

MICHAEL. About that. Now, I wanna be honest with you. The bank, we make loans to folks with no credit scores, we do, but ordinarily, we have a bit more income or more value in the home –

BOBBIE. So I might not get it?

MICHAEL. I'm going to talk to our Division Manager. Ask him to make an exception. I just want you to know it's not a guarantee that –

BOBBIE. I need this, Michael. I'm all out of options.

MICHAEL. Understood.

>   (**MICHAEL** *places the loan application in front of her.*)

You sign here.

BOBBIE. I have to sign?

MICHAEL. I can't submit the application without your signature.

>   (**BOBBIE** *signs.*)

>   (**DEBRA** *enters.* **MICHAEL** *quickly grabs and gathers up the papers that* **BOBBIE** *has just finished signing.*)

DEBRA. Michael. Luke.

MICHAEL. Hello there.

LUKE. Hey Debra.

DEBRA. Didn't expect to see you here.

BOBBIE. Michael and Luke were just stoppin' by to say hi.

DEBRA. It's awfully nice of you to drive all the way out here.

MICHAEL. Just wanted to come out for a visit, you know.

BOBBIE. Wanted to talk church stuff.

DEBRA. Well I know how much my mom enjoys discussing that. I'm sorry I haven't been in awhile.

MICHAEL. Actually, your mom called me this morning to tell me the good news.

DEBRA. Good news?

MICHAEL. Did she tell you? She's decided to join the church choir!

(**BOBBIE** *almost chokes.*)

DEBRA. Mom! I didn't know you wanted to go back to church!

BOBBIE. Yeah. Well, I do.

MICHAEL. Said she woke up this morning and decided today's the day.

BOBBIE. I woke up, and there was Jesus. Talkin' to me.

DEBRA. Wow.

MICHAEL. I'll see you two on Sunday.

DEBRA. Yes, see you Sunday.

BOBBIE. Bye.

(**MICHAEL** *and* **LUKE** *exit.*)

DEBRA. Thank you.

BOBBIE. You don't got to thank me.

DEBRA. You're finally gonna go to church with me.

BOBBIE. I never understood why you wanted to go to this church.

DEBRA. I know who I am. And I know there are parts of me this church doesn't accept. But I found something there. And I found it with Daddy.

> (**DEBRA** *and* **BOBBIE** *exit. In front of the house, on the porch, once* **LUKE** *is sure they are out of listening range distance.* **JANE** *enters and sits at her desk in her Manhattan office.*)

Eleven

> (**LUKE** *watches* **MICHAEL** *go, then takes out his cell phone and calls* **JANE**. **JANE** *looks at her phone, sees it's* **LUKE**. *She sends it to voicemail.* **LUKE**, *frustrated, dials* **JANE** *again. She answers.*)

JANE. Luke, I'm working.

LUKE. I know, I'm sorry, I just –

JANE. Everything okay?

LUKE. I just visited your mom –

JANE. Something wrong?

LUKE. Not, not immediately. But she's in a situation that –

JANE. Okay. Let's talk later. Alright? Sorry, I just, I have deadlines.

LUKE. Of course.

JANE. Thanks Luke.

> (**JANE** *hangs up on* **LUKE**. **LUKE** *exits.* **JANE** *resumes her work.*)

> (**PETER MINUIT** *enters, followed by* **JAKOB**.)

PETER MINUIT. Is this the one?

Twelve

(Manahatta.)

JAKOB. *(Points to* **JANE.***)* Yes.

PETER MINUIT. You're sure that's her?

JAKOB. I'm sure –

PETER MINUIT. They all look alike.

JAKOB. Le-le-wa'-you!

LE-LE-WA'-YOU. Jakob.

JAKOB. *(To* **PETER MINUIT.***)* This is the woman I mentioned.

PETER MINUIT. Introduce me.

JAKOB. Please, allow me to introduce Peter Minuit. Governor of the Dutch West India Company.

LE-LE-WA'-YOU. I'm pleased to meet you.

PETER MINUIT. She speaks!

JAKOB. Yes –

PETER MINUIT. A woman that speaks!

JAKOB. She's quite fluent. I told you, she's who I trade with now, along the Broad Way –

PETER MINUIT. How extraordinary.

(Turns to **LE-LE-WA'-YOU.***)*

I need to meet with your people.

LE-LE-WA'-YOU. You've come to the right place. This is our camp, and I'd be happy to introduce you to –

PETER MINUIT. Is your leader here?

*(**MOTHER, TOOSH-KI-PA-KWIS-I,** and **SE-KET-TU-MAY-QUA** enter to see what all the commotion is about.)*

MOTHER. We have guests?

LE-LE-WA'-YOU. These are the men I told you about. I trade with them.

PETER MINUIT. *(To* **SE-KET-TU-MAY-QUA**.*)* Are you the leader?

>   *(***SE-KET-TU-MAY-QUA** *isn't sure how to respond.)*

Are you the Director? The, the man who makes important decisions?

>   *(***SE-KET-TU-MAY-QUA** *isn't sure how to respond.)*

TOOSH-KI-PA-KWIS-I. What's he saying?

SE-KET-TU-MAY-QUA. He wants to know if I make important decisions.

PETER MINUIT. *(To* **JAKOB**.*)* Help me here.

(To **SE-KET-TU-MAY-QUA**.*)* Are you in charge?

SE-KET-TU-MAY-QUA. I am not.

PETER MINUIT. Dear God!

SE-KET-TU-MAY-QUA. Our women make the important decisions –

PETER MINUIT. *(To* **JAKOB**.*)* He speaks.

(To **SE-KET-TU-MAY-QUA**.*)* We're so thankful you can speak.

SE-KET-TU-MAY-QUA. As am I.

PETER MINUIT. Tell me, what is your name?

SE-KET-TU-MAY-QUA. Se-ket-tu-may-qua.

PETER MINUIT. Does that mean something?

SE-KET-TU-MAY-QUA. Yes, it's my name.

PETER MINUIT. No, but Indians have names that mean something.

SE-KET-TU-MAY-QUA. Black Beaver.

PETER MINUIT. Black Beaver?!

SE-KET-TU-MAY-QUA. That's my name. In your language.

PETER MINUIT. Oh marvelous. Black Beaver, we are here to discuss something very important.

(**PETER MINUIT** *extends his hand to* **MOTHER.**)

Hello there.

MOTHER. *(To* **LE-LE-WA'-YOU.***)* What does he want from me?

LE-LE-WA'-YOU. He wants to touch your hand.

MOTHER. I don't want to touch his.

LE-LE-WA'-YOU. *(To* **PETER MINUIT.***)* You'll have to excuse us. Some of us aren't accustomed to touching hands.

MOTHER. *(Gestures to the* **DUTCH.***)* Please. Welcome our guests.

PETER MINUIT. We're not interrupting anything are we?

LE-LE-WA'-YOU. We're preparing a meal.

MOTHER. Invite them to sit down.

LE-LE-WA'-YOU. We invite you to sit down.

MOTHER. Enjoy themselves.

LE-LE-WA'-YOU. We want you to enjoy yourselves.

PETER MINUIT. Oh, thank you. Tell me, Black Beaver, have you ever had brandy?

(**PETER MINUIT** *gestures to* **JAKOB,** *who pulls out glasses and a bottle of brandy.)*

SE-KET-TU-MAY-QUA. I'm not sure that I have.

PETER MINUIT. Well you absolutely must give it a try. This bottle is a fine, or rather, a great, indeed I think the greatest, spirit ever made.

(*JAKOB pours a glass for* **TOOSH-KI-PA-KWIS-I,** **MOTHER,** *and* **LE-LE-WA'-YOU** *as well.*)

MOTHER. *(To* **SE-KET-TU-MAY-QUA.***)* What is this?

SE-KET-TU-MAY-QUA. I'm not sure.

LE-LE-WA'-YOU. Something from their Great Spirit.

(**PETER MINUIT** *lifts his glass.*)

PETER MINUIT. To the New World!

(**PETER MINUIT** *leads them in an awkward toast, that the* **LENAPE** *do their best to emulate.*)

Well? What do you think?

(*They wince.*)

SE-KET-TU-MAY-QUA. *(To* **MOTHER.***)* He would like to know what you think.

MOTHER. It's different.

LE-LE-WA'-YOU. It's sweet.

TOOSH-KI-PA-KWIS-I. It's awful!

SE-KET-TU-MAY-QUA. *(To* **PETER MINUIT.***)* She finds it to be different.

PETER MINUIT. I knew she would like it! Please, have more!

(**JAKOB** *pours more into their glasses.*)

LE-LE-WA'-YOU. *(To her* **SISTER.***)* If you don't want yours, I'll finish it.

(**TOOSH-KI-PA-KWIS-I** *hands her* **SISTER** *her glass.*)

PETER MINUIT. Now, gentlemen, err ladies. Tell me. Do you own all of Manahatta?

LE-LE-WA'-YOU. Own?

PETER MINUIT. Does this land belong to you?

SE-KET-TU-MAY-QUA. We live here, yes.

PETER MINUIT. But does Manahatta belong to you?

SE-KET-TU-MAY-QUA. Manahatta?

PETER MINUIT. Isn't that what you call this island?

SE-KET-TU-MAY-QUA. Yes.

LE-LE-WA'-YOU. In your language that translates to the place we go to get the wood to make bows.

PETER MINUIT. Bows, like…

SE-KET-TU-MAY-QUA. For hunting.

PETER MINUIT. I see.

SE-KET-TU-MAY-QUA. We made our bows from the hickory trees on the southern tip of the island –

PETER MINUIT. Hickory. That's a tree? I don't believe I've ever seen one.

SE-KET-TU-MAY-QUA. You chopped them all down.

LE-LE-WA'-YOU. Manahatta is the word our ancestors used to describe their home.

PETER MINUIT. This place?

SE-KET-TU-MAY-QUA. This island.

LE-LE-WA'-YOU. Manahatta.

SE-KET-TU-MAY-QUA. Our home.

PETER MINUIT. So you own Manahatta.

SE-KET-TU-MAY-QUA. If you say so.

PETER MINUIT. Not me, you. You just said it's your home.

Look, let's not overly complicate things. This is all very simple. The Dutch, my people, would like to trade with you and your people for Manahatta. You own Manahatta because it is your home.

MOTHER. What is he saying?

LE-LE-WA'-YOU. *(To* **MOTHER.***)* They wish to continue to trade with us here on Manahatta, our home.

PETER MINUIT. Think of it this way. If you agree to trade Manahatta, we're prepared to give you six knives, three axes, twelve kettles, and six guns.

SE-KET-TU-MAY-QUA. *(To* **MOTHER.***)* They wish to trade knives, axes –

LE-LE-WA'-YOU. Guns.

SE-KET-TU-MAY-QUA. Kettles.

JAKOB. Sir?

PETER MINUIT. Yes?

JAKOB. The gift.

PETER MINUIT. Oh, the gift.

(**JAKOB** *presents a wampum belt.)*

SE-KET-TU-MAY-QUA. What's this?

PETER MINUIT. We give this now to show our thanks. If it had not been for the food that your people gave us during our first winter here, we would have starved to death.

MOTHER. *(To* **SE-KET-TU-MAY-QUA.***)* This is authentic.

PETER MINUIT. *(To* **SE-KET-TU-MAY-QUA.***)* What did she say?

SE-KET-TU-MAY-QUA. This is real wampum.

PETER MINUIT. Wonderful, now tell me, will you agree to trade Manahatta?

MOTHER. *(To* **PETER MINUIT.***)* To the Lenape, when we gift wampum, that makes us family. Now we're related.

> (**MOTHER** *extends her hand to* **PETER MINUIT.** **PETER MINUIT** *quickly grabs her hand and gives it a hearty shake.)*

> (**PETER MINUIT** *looks to* **JAKOB** *with shock and amazement, and then laughs.)*

PETER MINUIT. We own Manahatta!

JAKOB. Incredible!

> (**PETER MINUIT** *snaps his fingers, and* **JAKOB** *pulls out a large piece of paper. He hands it to* **PETER MINUIT.***)*

SE-KET-TU-MAY-QUA. What's this?

PETER MINUIT. A deed. You sign here.

SE-KET-TU-MAY-QUA. I have to sign?

PETER MINUIT. Yes. This is a permanent trade –

SE-KET-TU-MAY-QUA. We'll trade forever?

PETER MINUIT. Sure. But first you must sign.

> (**LE-LE-WA'-YOU** *interjects and explains to her* **FAMILY.***)*

LE-LE-WA'-YOU. I've seen them do this. It's really quite simple.

> (*She looks to* **JAKOB**, *who nods. She turns back to her* **FAMILY.***)*

We all just leave a mark.

*(**LE-LE-WA'-YOU** takes the quill and marks an "x" on the deed. She hands the quill to **SE-KET-TU-MAY-QUA**, who does the same. He hands the pen to **MOTHER**, who does the same. Then **TOOSH-KI-PA-KWIS-I**.)*

*(**PETER MINUIT** turns to **JAKOB**, raising his glass to his.)*

PETER MINUIT. To Manahatta!

JAKOB. To Manahatta!

*(**LE-LE-WA'-YOU** does not understand the formality but is eager to emulate.)*

LE-LE-WA'-YOU. To Manahatta!

*(**LE-LE-WA'-YOU** and **PETER MINUIT** clink glasses.)*

*(**MICHAEL** enters and speaks to **MOTHER**.)*

MOTHER. Anyone who calls Manahatta home must know, the Creator gave us Manahatta.

MICHAEL. We need to talk.

MOTHER. Now Manahatta is your home.

MICHAEL. You've missed three payments.

Thirteen

(Anadarko.)

*(**MICHAEL** visits **BOBBIE** in her home. He hands **BOBBIE** an envelope. Everyone else exits.)*

BOBBIE. I don't understand how they got so high.

MICHAEL. You made your payments for the first year.

BOBBIE. I used everything I have, but now I, I can't keep up.

MICHAEL. We can put you on a special repayment plan. After that, it's foreclosure.

(Beat.)

BOBBIE. Maybe I get a second job.

MICHAEL. You said you work nights at Riverside?

BOBBIE. So a day job.

MICHAEL. What about the tribe's gas station?

BOBBIE. Already asked. You hiring anyone at the church?

MICHAEL. Not at the moment –

BOBBIE. You really wanted me there. I guess now you don't?

MICHAEL. I know I forced you to go to church. When Debra walked in that day, it was like I didn't even think about it, the words, they just came out.

BOBBIE. I noticed.

MICHAEL. You don't have to come no more.

BOBBIE. Ya don't want me to sing in the choir?

MICHAEL. No, you have a beautiful voice –

BOBBIE. If ya don't want me to sing in the choir, just say it.

MICHAEL. I want you there. In the choir. Charlie, and me, we'd been trying to get you there for years. He'd be mad if he knew I tricked you.

BOBBIE. I never understood why Charlie wanted to go to yer church. Or why he wanted to sing in your choir. I just knew I couldn't. But the other day, when I went back, when I sang in that choir, something happened. I don't know what, but I could hear him. Charlie, he was singin'. And then I heard my mom. My dad. All of 'em singin'. In Lenape.

And that's when I realized, my ancestors, my relations, they never stopped singin'. I stopped listenin'.

MICHAEL. I'm gonna do whatever I can to help you with this repayment plan. Bobbie, we're gonna make this work.

Fourteen

(Manhattan. **JOE** *enters Jane's office.)*

JANE. Sending to S&P now.

JOE. Now? They should have had this report five hours ago.

JANE. I know. I just, I had to double check the numbers –

JOE. Check the numbers?

JANE. I'm on the last paragraph.

JOE. Snake. I need this to be good, not perfect.

JANE. I know. Five minutes. I promise. It's late, you should go and I'll –

JOE. Copy me on the email.

JANE. Of course.

> *(***JOE*** fist bumps* **JANE** *and exits. Panicked,* **JANE** *returns to her work, typing as fast as she can. This report isn't nearly done.* **LUKE** *enters.)*

LUKE. Hey.

JANE. Oh, hey –

LUKE. It's ten. Actually, it's seven past ten –

JANE. I know. I told you to come get me.

LUKE. At ten.

JANE. I got behind. Give me fifteen. I'll be done in fifteen. I promise –

LUKE. You all have secretaries at night?

JANE. One during the day. A different one at night.

LUKE. She offered me coffee.

JANE. She's supposed to.

LUKE. At night?

JANE. What'd you do today?

LUKE. Took a walk down Pearl Street.

JANE. Tell my mom. She'd be thrilled.

LUKE. You should go. Just take a walk –

JANE. I don't have time –

LUKE. You work too much.

JANE. Save me the speech.

LUKE. Hey, you know, I got a promotion. They made me head of Loan Sales.

JANE. That's awesome.

LUKE. I'm in charge of all the loans we originate.

JANE. So you're busy.

LUKE. Dad says this is the most he's ever seen. We're doing ten, fifteen, sometimes twenty a month.

JANE. In Anadarko?

LUKE. We could work together.

JANE. On what?

LUKE. On securities. I'm head of Loan Sales.

JANE. That doesn't mean you know how to securitize them.

LUKE. How hard can it be?

JANE. It's not that simple.

(**LUKE** *picks up the phone.*)

LUKE. Hello. Would you like to buy a security?

JANE. That is not how it works –

LUKE. Two? Three? Two times three is six. Why don't you buy six? Did I mention I love math?

JANE. You aren't using the right language –

LUKE. ABS. CDO. ABS. CDO. Tranche. Tranche. ABS. CDO. Tranche. Tranche. ABS. CDO. Tranche. Tranche. Tranche. Tranche.

(**JANE** *laughs.*)

Jane. There's something I need to tell you.

JANE. Yeah, okay.

LUKE. It's about your dad, and his surgery –

JANE. I know I wasn't there, and some people will never forgive me for that. But I have to move on. Life keeps going and I'm not –

LUKE. That's not, you know me, Jane, I've never once judged you for that. But there are things you don't know –

JANE. Like what?

LUKE. When your dad needed that surgery, IHS, they refused to –

(**JOE** *enters.*)

JANE. I'm sending the report to S&P now –

JOE. You said that ten minutes ago.

JANE. I know, but I –

JOE. (*Sees* **LUKE**.) Who's this guy?

JANE. My friend. From Oklahoma. He's visiting.

JOE. That's precious.

LUKE. (*Tries to shake* **JOE**'s *hand.*) I'm Luke.

(**JOE** *doesn't accept the shake.*)

JOE. I don't understand why you're standing here.

JANE. He wanted to see what it's like, you know, trading on Wall Street.

JOE. *(To* **LUKE**.*)* Everyone thinks they wanna be here. But very few have what it takes.

(*To* **JANE**, *gesturing to* **LUKE**.*)* This is why you're not working.

JANE. I've been working –

JOE. On what? Ten minutes Snake. S&P better have that report.

(**JOE** *exits.)*

JANE. I told you. I have to finish this.

LUKE. Sorry I interrupted.

JANE. No, wait –

LUKE. I get it. You're busy.

JANE. I'm the first Native, ever, that I know of, that you know of, that anyone knows to work on Wall Street.

LUKE. You're a big deal.

JANE. I can't afford to fail. If I do, I close the door on everyone who might come behind me.

LUKE. You think the door's open?

JANE. It's about opportunities, and creating them –

LUKE. If you succeed, they won't open the door for me. Or anyone else from our community. They'll say you're the exception.

JANE. I'd rather be the exception than a failure.

LUKE. All your dad ever wanted was to visit Pearl Street. You've been here four years, and you don't have time to walk down it.

Fifteen

(Manhattan. Present Day.)

*(Same time. **JOE** and **DICK** enter Joe's office.)*

JOE. Eight-seven, Dick, we're at eighty-seven!

DICK. Somebody's in a good mood today.

JOE. We just keep climbing.

DICK. You secured Shaw yet?

JOE. He's talking to J.P. Morgan.

DICK. Are you fucking serious?

JOE. He won't return my calls.

DICK. Pin him down. We're not losing Shaw to fucking J.P. Morgan. Hey, you like Manhattans?

JOE. Been known to drink 'em a time or two.

DICK. Gotta get Kathy's dad a birthday present, and I know he loves Manhattans.

JOE. Bourbon or rye?

DICK. That's what I gotta figure out. I can't get him the wrong thing, I'll never hear the end of it.

JOE. In that case, go with Van Winkle.

DICK. There's a reason I rely on you for salient advice.

(Picks up sheet of paper from Joe's desk.)

OK, who's at the top of your low deals list this month?

JOE. Jane Snake.

DICK. I didn't realize we paid people to prevent deals from closing.

JOE. It's my fault. I thought she had what it takes, and it turns out she doesn't. I tried talking to her, but clearly that didn't work.

DICK. It's no fun firing someone you've hired, but... What's wrong? You like this one?

JOE. No. I mean, not like that. I thought she had potential.

DICK. Let me do the talking.

WOMAN'S VOICE. *(From speakerphone.)* Jane Snake here to see you.

DICK. Send her in.

>   *(**JANE** enters.)*

JANE. If this is about the RALI deal, they never sent us the final loan tape –

DICK. This isn't about RALI.

JANE. Oh.

DICK. You're on the low deals list.

JANE. I'm sorry?

JOE. You need to close a few more deals each month.

DICK. A LOT more.

JOE. And I'm sure you have an explanation –

DICK. But we don't care to hear it.

JOE. What he means to say is that we want to help you do your best –

DICK. Would you lay off the Cool Whip?

JOE. I'm trying to explain –

DICK. Get me a cup of coffee.

JOE. You want coffee?

DICK. I want you to shut the fuck up and bring me some Starbucks.

JOE. You don't drink Starbucks.

DICK. I do now. Bring me back a mocha latte venti frappé.

JOE. They, that's not, they don't have that.

DICK. Fine. Call me when you get there and I'll tell you what I want.

JOE. Why don't I just ask Shirley to make an espresso here –

DICK. Because you need to take a walk. And I need to talk to Janet.

(**JOE** *exits.*)

Alright Janet, you should know this low deals list is serious business.

JANE. I can explain.

DICK. You're not closing enough deals.

JANE. I'm closing five or six each month –

DICK. You're on the low deals list.

JANE. I'll close more deals.

DICK. Much more.

JANE. How much do you think is enough?

DICK. There's no such thing as enough on Wall Street. You're fired.

JANE. Fired?

DICK. Done. Finito. You failed.

(*Dick's BlackBerry rings.*)

Dick Fuld... Are you serious?

(*Pulls phone away.*)

DICK. Fucking Goldman, trying to fuck us out of our own deal. I gotta take this.

> (**DICK** *starts to exit.*)

(To **JANE** *as he exits.)* Nice knowing you, Janet.

(As he exits, into the BlackBerry.) What the fuck Jimmy?

> (**JANE** *sits in Joe's office. She looks around, confirms no one is in sight. She opens up a drawer, pulls out a notepad. Reads what's written. Picks up the phone and dials a number.)*

JANE. Yes, I'm calling for Mr. Shaw... Jane Snake, with J.P. Morgan. Thank you.

> *(She waits a moment, and then –)*

Mr. Shaw, Jane Snake here, if you have a moment – J.P. Morgan? Oh no, I'm with Lehman. She said J.P. Morgan? Are you, oh no, please tell me you aren't purchasing notes in one of their doubly synthetic CDOs... Well, uh, how do I put this nicely. Those notes aren't worth the paper they're written on. Forget J.P. Morgan. Forget the structure. You want to focus on the tranche.

Equity? Well thank god you didn't purchase that... Never. Do me a favor and don't give equity a second thought...

Because that's the first tranche to go. Sure, it's got the biggest returns right now, but the first defaults to come in the door flood out all of the equity holders... You want to buy the sweet spot, just below the mezzanine, but right above the equity. It's a hybrid-tranche, really. And most investors overlook it. And believe me, when you call J.P. Morgan, they're not gonna give you the sweet spot. They don't know where to find it...

You want three hundred? OK yes, of course. I'll tell Joe. Me? Jane Snake. Oh. I'm his Senior Vice President. Of? Structured Finance. Yes, Mr. Shaw thank you…yes, until next time.

(**JANE** *hangs up.* **JOE** *enters, carrying three coffees.*)

JOE. OK, so I got your coffee – where's Dick?

JANE. I don't know, he had to take a call. Something about Goldman. And Mike called for you. So I spoke to him.

JOE. Mike Shaw?

JANE. I convinced him to buy three hundred.

JOE. Three hundred?

JANE. He wants to buy three hundred thousand dollars worth of RMBS notes –

JOE. Million.

JANE. What?

JOE. You can't close a securitization to save your life, but you just convinced Mike Shaw to buy three hundred million from one of our bullshit CDOs. I've been trying to do that for weeks.

JANE. I can sell securities to people. That's easy. I just can't figure out how to close due diligence on a loan pool with no loan tape and thousands of missing files –

JOE. You're too much of a perfectionist.

JANE. I really don't like transaction management –

JOE. We have you in the wrong job –

JANE. I want to trade.

JOE. And trade you shall!

JANE. I lied to him.

JOE. What?

JANE. I told him that I'm your Senior Vice President.

JOE. Of what?

JANE. Structured Finance.

JOE. That position doesn't exist!

JANE. I know.

JOE. Shaw is one of our most important clients –

JANE. I know. And.

JOE. And what?

JANE. Dick fired me.

JOE. Fuck. Of course he did.

> *(Beat.)*

Alright Snake, here's what I'm gonna do. I'm creating a new position, Senior Vice President of Structured Finance. That's you. You work for me. Directly.

JANE. Thank you.

JOE. No need to thank me. Putting talent in the right place is my job. Oh, and Snake. I want to apologize, you know, some of the things I've said since you got here –

JANE. Oh, no, really, it's fine –

JOE. It's not fine. Just because I'm ignorant doesn't mean I should get to say whatever the hell I want without ever thinking about it. That's why I like having you around Snake. You make me think. This world, it's changing. It's like it's expanding and contracting. At the same time. We need you Snake. Don't ever forget that.

Sixteen

(Anadarko, Bobbie's home. Thanksgiving 2007.)

*(**DEBRA** sits at the living room table in front of a pile of peeled potatoes. **JANE** stands, suitcase in hand, carrying a large sack of groceries in a Whole Foods bag.*)*

DEBRA. What are you doing here?

JANE. Mom didn't tell you I was coming?

DEBRA. Nope.

JANE. Oh. Well, sorry I'm late. They canceled the only direct to OKC and I had to connect through Dallas. You making dinner?

DEBRA. Dinner don't make itself.

*(**JANE** nods.)*

JANE. I'd love to help. I have to go back tomorrow, but while I'm here –

DEBRA. Tomorrow?

JANE. At least they gave me Thanksgiving off.

DEBRA. That's nice of them, you know, since it's a sacred Indigenous holiday.

*(**JANE** smiles at her sister's sarcasm.)*

JANE. They asked me what we do to celebrate. I told them we sacrifice a buffalo.

*(**JANE** sets her Whole Foods bag of groceries down.)*

---

* A license to produce *Manahatta* does not include a license to publicly display any branded logos or trademarked images. Licensees must acquire rights for any logos and/or images or create their own.

DEBRA. What's this?

> (**DEBRA** *pulls out a large green leafy item.*)

JANE. I brought some kale.

> (**DEBRA** *stares.*)

I thought maybe this year we could make it, you know, instead.

DEBRA. Of what?

JANE. Frybread.

DEBRA. Are you serious?

JANE. It's very nutritious.

DEBRA. No way you're gonna get Mom to eat kale.

JANE. I can try.

> (*Beat.*)

You're making potatoes?

DEBRA. I bought 'em at Half Foods.

JANE. Can I help?

> (**DEBRA** *hands her a potato peeler.*)

DEBRA. <u>Pxa kho nek hopenisak</u> (Peel the potatoes.)

JANE. You know I don't speak Lenape.

DEBRA. Peel the potatoes.

> (*The* **SISTERS** *peel.*)

JANE. So. You still dating, oh sorry, what was her name?

DEBRA. Carla?

JANE. The Comanche you met in Lawton?

DEBRA. God no.

JANE. Oh, sorry.

DEBRA. Don't be. I'm not.

JANE. Judi's with Randy's cousin.

DEBRA. Everyone's dating a Kiowa. Pretty soon there won't be any Delaware Lenape. We'll all be Kiowa.

JANE. So date a Lenape.

DEBRA. Right. And where do you suggest I find one? That we're not related to?

JANE. The City?

DEBRA. I left the City. To move in with Mom.

JANE. I know.

DEBRA. You don't. Jane. You have no idea what I've had to give up.

(*Beat.*)

Luke came by the other day. Wanted to know when you might be back.

JANE. What'd you tell him?

DEBRA. The truth. That you never come home anymore. That we never see you.

(*They peel potatoes.*)

You met anyone in Manhattan yet?

JANE. Oh, no. I mean, not yet. But I'm sure I will, you know. Eventually.

DEBRA. I'm sure it's hard to meet people when you work all the time.

(**BOBBIE** *enters with a pile of paperwork in her hands.*)

BOBBIE. I found my résumé.

JANE. Hey Mom.

(**BOBBIE** *hugs her* **DAUGHTER.**)

BOBBIE. Janie. When'd you get here?

JANE. Just now.

(**DEBRA** *comes to the table, carrying potatoes.*)

DEBRA. She's gotta go back tomorrow.

BOBBIE. Guess they're still workin' ya hard.

JANE. *(Seeing the paperwork in* **BOBBIE**'s *hands.)* Are you applying for a new job?

DEBRA. ANA grant. For language classes.

JANE. *(To* **BOBBIE.**) You're going to teach?

BOBBIE. If we get it.

JANE. Mom! That's amazing!

(**BOBBIE** *regards the kale.*)

BOBBIE. What's that?

JANE. Kale.

BOBBIE. Smells like horse poo.

JANE. It's very nutritious. Lots of vitamins and minerals.

BOBBIE. Huh.

JANE. Oh, and Mom, I finally took a walk down Pearl Street, where we used to collect shells. I've been thinking about what you said. So I did some research online, and I –

BOBBIE. Ya can't trust the internets.

JANE. I had no idea that the Broad Way, Broadway, was our trading trail, you know, with our relatives up north. They named it after us!

BOBBIE. The whole island's named after us.

(**BOBBIE** *turns back to her paperwork.*)

Why you schedulin' class for Thursday nights?

DEBRA. We have to show them we have it all planned out, you know, every single detail –

BOBBIE. I work Thursday night.

DEBRA. So ask for the night off.

BOBBIE. It's my job, Debra.

DEBRA. You're senior enough by now, they should give you the day shift.

BOBBIE. I like the night shift.

DEBRA. You do not.

BOBBIE. I get paid extra to work the night shift, and I can't give it up.

DEBRA. Don't forget to sign this one.

(**DEBRA** *hands a form to* **BOBBIE.**)

BOBBIE. This makes no sense.

DEBRA. It's the Objective Work Plan –

BOBBIE. What kinda report am I supposed to give on a quarterly basis?

DEBRA. ANA won't fund us unless we give them deliverables.

BOBBIE. What the hell is a deliverable.

DEBRA. You know, achievements. They want to see that we're using the federal funds they give us to create tangible benefits.

BOBBIE. It's a language. Not a widget factory.

DEBRA. I'll just say the students in your class will learn fifty words a week. So that's two hundred words a month –

BOBBIE. You don't learn Lenape in a month.

DEBRA. I know –

BOBBIE. I grew up listenin' to Lenape, for years. Ya don't learn it overnight.

JANE. Remember the day Dad convinced the Council to create the language program and apply for the ANA grant.

Only vote in the history of our Nation that got a unanimous yes.

He was so excited.

DEBRA. He walked in this front door, turned to us, smiled and said: <u>Nulhatenami</u> <u>Weli kishku</u> (I am happy. It is a good day.)

JANE. He was in tears.

DEBRA. *(Mispronounces it.)* <u>Nkaski alenixsi</u> (I can speak Lenape.)

JANE. What does that mean?

DEBRA. I can speak Lenape.

(Mispronounces it.) <u>Nkaski alenixsi</u>

BOBBIE. *(Is one hundred percent accurate, corrects her daughter.)* <u>Nkaski alenixsi</u>

DEBRA. *(Tries again but mispronounces it.)* <u>Nkaski alenixsi</u>

BOBBIE. How the hell you gonna teach Lenape when ya ain't got a clue how to say it?

JANE. Mom.

BOBBIE. Take me off the application.

*(**BOBBIE** exits.)*

JANE. You could teach.

DEBRA. I'm not fluent.

JANE. We have other speakers.

DEBRA. Who do you know that speaks?

JANE. Harry's uncle.

DEBRA. Dead.

JANE. Grandma Lilly.

DEBRA. Died two years ago. You've been gone a long time.

> (**JANE** *reaches into her purse and pulls out her checkbook. She writes a check and hands it to* **DEBRA.**)

What's this?

JANE. Enough to get you started.

> (**DEBRA** *returns the check to* **JANE.**)

DEBRA. I can't run a language program without any speakers.

JANE. You speak. You've just convinced yourself that you don't.

> (**JANE** *hands the check back to* **DEBRA** *who accepts.* **JAKOB** *enters and approaches* **JANE.**)

JAKOB. How many do you have?

Seventeen

(Manahatta. Late spring.)

*(***LE-LE-WA'-YOU*** *hands the furs to* **JAKOB**.*)*

LE-LE-WA'-YOU. Five.

JAKOB. They're beautiful.

LE-LE-WA'-YOU. Thank you.

JAKOB. I'll pay you forty guilders, for your whole load.

LE-LE-WA'-YOU. Guilders, but not wampum?

JAKOB. Company has instructed us to trade in guilders, no more wampum.

LE-LE-WA'-YOU. I see.

JAKOB. Is forty enough?

LE-LE-WA'-YOU. Yes.

*(***JAKOB*** *hands her the guilders.)*

JAKOB. <u>Weli kishku.</u> (It is a good day.)

LE-LE-WA'-YOU. Until next time.

(Realizes she's missing five.)

Jakob – I think you made a mistake. You only gave me thirty-five.

JAKOB. Right.

LE-LE-WA'-YOU. We agreed on forty. I'm missing five.

JAKOB. That's the tax.

LE-LE-WA'-YOU. What is tax?

JAKOB. The price you pay to trade on the Company's land.

*(***JAKOB*** *exits.)*

Eighteen

(Manahatta. Lenape encampment. **JONAS MICHAELIUS** *enters to find* **TOOSH-KI-PA-KWIS-I***.)*

JONAS MICHAELIUS. Hello. I would like to tell you about Jesus Christ, our Lord and Savior. Our congregation, we're up to forty-two. Lenape from all over the island. But I've never seen you. Would you like to come to church?

Perhaps you don't speak.

TOOSH-KI-PA-KWIS-I. <u>Keku hech kteluwensi</u> (What is your name)?

JONAS MICHAELIUS. Would you like to sing?

*(***TOOSH-KI-PA-KWIS-I** *smiles at him out of pity.)*

One of our Lenape helped me translate a song into your language. It's a simple hymn, really. But one of my favorites.

(He pulls out a piece of paper.)

(Singing.)

NO-WA-TONE, NO-WA-TONE,
HAY-LAY-LOIEMA, GEE-SHAY-LOIEMA.

*(***TOOSH-KI-PA-KWIS-I** *laughs at his pronunciation.)*

TOOSH-KI-PA-KWIS-I. *(She corrects his pronunciation.)* <u>No-wa-tone</u>

JONAS MICHAELIUS. *(Tries to imitate her.)* <u>No-wa-tone?</u>

TOOSH-KI-PA-KWIS-I. *(Nods with approval.)* <u>No-wa-tone</u>.

JONAS MICHAELIUS. <u>Hay-lay-loiema, gee-shay-loiema.</u>

    (**TOOSH-KI-PA-KWIS-I** *corrects his pronunciation.*)

JONAS MICHAELIUS. *(Correctly.)* <u>Loiema?</u>

TOOSH-KI-PA-KWIS-I. <u>Gee-shay loiema</u>

    (Together, they sing.)

JONAS MICHAELIUS & TOOSH-KI-PA-KWIS-I. *(Singing.)*
NO-WA-TONE, NO-WA-TONE,
HAY-LAY-LOIEMA, GEE-SHAY-LOIEMA.
NO-WA-TONE, NO-WA-TONE,
HAY-LAY-LOIEMA, GEE-SHAY-LOIEMA.

    (**SE-KET-TU-MAY-QUA** *enters and points his gun at* **JONAS MICHAELIUS.**)

TOOSH-KI-PA-KWIS-I. <u>Ku ta!</u> (No)!

JONAS MICHAELIUS. Don't shoot!

SE-KET-TU-MAY-QUA. What are you doing here?

JONAS MICHAELIUS. I have good news.

SE-KET-TU-MAY-QUA. The Dutch ended their fur tax?

JONAS MICHAELIUS. No. You are forgiven. Our Lord and Savior, Jesus Christ, has died for your sins.

SE-KET-TU-MAY-QUA. That doesn't sound like good news.

JONAS MICHAELIUS. The Dutch West India Company sent me here to start the first church in New Amsterdam.

SE-KET-TU-MAY-QUA. You're with the Company?

JONAS MICHAELIUS. Yes –

SE-KET-TU-MAY-QUA. You need to leave. Now. Or I'll shoot –

JONAS MICHAELIUS. I come in peace –

SE-KET-TU-MAY-QUA. I will shoot you.

(*Terrified,* **JONAS MICHAELIUS** *backs away, and then turns and runs offstage.*)

TOOSH-KI-PA-KWIS-I. (*Re: his gun.*) Put that down.

SE-KET-TU-MAY-QUA. Do you have any idea what you're doing?

TOOSH-KI-PA-KWIS-I. We were singing.

SE-KET-TU-MAY-QUA. He's with the Company.

TOOSH-KI-PA-KWIS-I. That man will never harm anyone –

SE-KET-TU-MAY-QUA. They killed your cousins.

(*Beat.*)

I found them. Across the trail, this morning. By the water to the west. They were fishing. The Dutch showed up with guns and shot them all. Men, women, children. Only Ope Luwan survived. I found her, hiding in a tree.

(**TOOSH-KI-PA-KWIS-I** *collapses.*)

(**SE-KET-TU-MAY-QUA** *puts his gun in her arms.*)

If you see any white man enter our encampment, shoot.

(**MICHAEL** *enters and approaches* **SE-KET-TU-MAY-QUA**.)

MICHAEL. I need you to take Bobbie Snake this letter.

Nineteen

(Anadarko. February 2008.)

MICHAEL. I told her you'd be free tomorrow. I'll be in the City, so I'm sending you.

(**MICHAEL** *hands* **LUKE** *a letter.*)

(**TOOSH-KI-PA-KWIS-I** *exits.*)

LUKE. *(Stares at the letter.)* This is a foreclosure notice.

MICHAEL. We've done all that we can.

LUKE. No, no. We haven't.

MICHAEL. Really? What do you suggest?

LUKE. We can restructure the loan –

MICHAEL. We tried that.

LUKE. But the repayment plan –

MICHAEL. Isn't going to get better. The penalties, they're stacking up, and at this point, there are just no, we have no options.

LUKE. But the bank –

MICHAEL. Is done. They've been patient, unbelievably patient. For six years I've convinced them to keep this loan on their balance sheet, I know that's what you wanted. It's what I wanted. I wanted to help Bobbie. But she's not gonna pay. She can't. Not now. Not tomorrow. Not six weeks from now. The bank is ready to foreclose.

LUKE. Jane could pay the balance in a heartbeat –

MICHAEL. Probably.

LUKE. I could call her –

MICHAEL. But you won't. You promised Bobbie.

LUKE. That was before she went into default –

MICHAEL. Bobbie doesn't have much in the world. But she has her dignity. I know you wouldn't want to take that from her. Besides, you don't need to be calling Jane no more. I wanna introduce you to Carl's niece –

LUKE. I met Jenny. She's nice.

MICHAEL. Mike, the pastor over in Lawton –

LUKE. Has a daughter that I'm not gonna date. I'm not calling Jane to ask her on a date, I'm calling her because her mom is about to lose her home –

MICHAEL. You told Bobbie you wouldn't.

LUKE. And I haven't. I would never break a promise with an elder. But this… Don't go to the City. Come with me.

MICHAEL. You have to do this.

LUKE. Alone?

MICHAEL. This is part of the job. Loan sales isn't just sales. Sometimes there are defaults. And we handle both.

> *(Beat.)*

When you came into my care, you'd been living with your grandparents, who if I recall, hardly spoke a word of English. You'd been living in a home where Christ was nothing more than a foreign concept. I've worked hard to provide for you. To give you an education. And introduce you to our Savior.

You've come so far. I'm so proud of you. You're ready for this. I wouldn't ask you to do it if I thought you weren't.

> **(PETER MINUIT** *enters and speaks to* **MICHAEL.***)*

PETER MINUIT. I wish you the best on your journey.

Twenty

(Manahatta.)

*(**PETER MINUIT** sits at his desk. **JONAS MICHAELIUS** waves a letter.)*

JONAS MICHAELIUS. They're sending me back. On the next ship.

PETER MINUIT. That's unfortunate.

JONAS MICHAELIUS. You told them to remove me from my post.

PETER MINUIT. I told them their pastor was not acting in the best interests of the Company.

JONAS MICHAELIUS. How can you say that?

PETER MINUIT. You told the Indians to stop trading fur.

JONAS MICHAELIUS. Because you instructed your men to shoot them.

PETER MINUIT. Only if they refuse to pay the tax.

JONAS MICHAELIUS. And now they won't come to church.

PETER MINUIT. They need to pay the tax.

JONAS MICHAELIUS. Your tax has prevented them from coming to church.

PETER MINUIT. My tax pays for your godforsaken church!

JONAS MICHAELIUS. I pray for your soul.

PETER MINUIT. I don't doubt that you do.

JONAS MICHAELIUS. Matthew 6, verse 24. "No one can serve two masters. Either you will hate the one and love the other" –

PETER MINUIT. I don't read scripture.

JONAS MICHAELIUS. "You cannot serve both God and money."

PETER MINUIT. You can quote Jesus all you want Jonas, but at the end of the day, do you know who pays for your church? Fur and tulips. Not Indians sitting in pews. Fur and tulips.

JONAS MICHAELIUS. Your tulip is worthless. The tulip bubble burst.

PETER MINUIT. Tell me, what does Jesus have to say about that?

> (**JAKOB** *enters. He and* **JONAS MICHAELIUS** *regard one another. Defeated,* **JONAS MICHAELIUS** *exits.)*

JAKOB. Seven. Today, sir. And just yesterday they shot five –

PETER MINUIT. Where?

JAKOB. Along the Broad Way, where they come to –

PETER MINUIT. We need more guns.

JAKOB. I think we should stop shooting them.

PETER MINUIT. They're shooting us.

JAKOB. Because we're shooting them.

PETER MINUIT. You said they would pay the tax.

JAKOB. That was my hope.

PETER MINUIT. You said they'd come around. That they're dependent upon us to trade, now, and eventually they'd give up this nonsense and just pay the tax.

JAKOB. I was wrong. And I promise you, they'll never pay the tax if we keep shooting them.

PETER MINUIT. So what do you suggest?

JAKOB. We cease fire. We lift the tax –

PETER MINUIT. Absolutely not. Never.

JAKOB. Temporarily, for a short time –

PETER MINUIT. We will never lift the tax.

JAKOB. We should try to talk to them.

PETER MINUIT. No one gets to live here for free.

JAKOB. We can't, the Company, we're a group of traders. We're not prepared for warfare.

PETER MINUIT. I'll secure more guns.

JAKOB. We have a very small militia.

PETER MINUIT. How small?

JAKOB. Less than a hundred men at this point.

PETER MINUIT. Good god.

JAKOB. They're attacking us, now, from all sides. We desperately need reinforcements.

PETER MINUIT. Make an announcement. For every redskin that a colonist brings in, the Company'll pay an award.

JAKOB. With what? The Company has no capital. All we have is debt.

PETER MINUIT. Wampum. We'll pay the award in wampum... Do you think ten fathoms is enough?

> (**JANE** *enters.*)

JANE. You asked to see me.

Twenty-One

(Manhattan. Present day.)

*(**DICK** and **JOE** stand in Dick's office. **JOE** hands **DICK** a sheet of paper. He looks at the paper, then looks at **JANE**.)*

DICK. This the same girl that was on the low deals list?

JOE. One and the same.

DICK. The girl I fired and you rehired?

JOE. One and only.

DICK. Did you sleep with her?

JOE. No!

DICK. Good.

JANE. If it's the Credit Suisse deal, I can explain.

JOE. No –

JANE. The CDO is doubly-synthetic.

JOE. Snake –

JANE. So it owns a swap referenced in the collateral, as opposed to the securities themselves.

DICK. Good God. This has nothing to do with Credit Suisse.

(Waves a piece of paper.)

Do you know what this is?

JANE. No.

DICK. It's a printout. I see a list of names here. In the last six months, no one in the RMBS Group has brought in more investors than Jane Snake. Jane Snake, is that you?

JANE. Yes.

DICK. Congratulations.

JOE. You've been promoted.

DICK. To Executive Vice President of Capital Markets.

JANE. Thank you.

JOE. Keep it up, Snake.

> (**DICK** *hands* **JANE** *an envelope.*)

JANE. What's this?

DICK. Your bonus.

> (**JANE** *opens the envelope containing her million dollar bonus.*)

Welcome to the Management Team, Snake.

Twenty-Two

(**LUKE** *walks to Bobbie's front door. He goes to knock. He hesitates. He goes to knock again, but instead, takes out his phone and calls* **JANE**. *It clicks to voicemail.*)

JANE'S VOICEMAIL. *(Voice-over.)* Hello. You've reached the voicemail of Jane Snake, Executive Vice President of Capital Markets. Leave your name and number, or dial three–two–five for assistance.

(*Beep.*)

LUKE. Uh, hey Jane. It's Luke. You should, uh, call your mom.

(*He hangs up.* **BOBBIE** *appears at her front door.*)

BOBBIE. I thought I heard you out here. Come on in.

(*He does.*)

Can I get you some coffee?

LUKE. I'm fine.

BOBBIE. Have a seat.

LUKE. I can't stay long.

BOBBIE. You know how much these monthly payments are?

LUKE. The bank noticed your home for foreclosure.

BOBBIE. You're gonna sell my home?

LUKE. This is the notice.

(**BOBBIE** *collapses into her seat.*)

BOBBIE. I have to tell the girls.

(*Beat.*)

LUKE. You want me to call Debra?

BOBBIE. No.

LUKE. I know you didn't want to tell her, before, but now –

BOBBIE. She won't understand.

LUKE. She might, if you just –

BOBBIE. *(Waves foreclosure notice.)* You gave me a notice. I got time. Auction hasn't been set yet.

LUKE. No, but it will be –

BOBBIE. I'll figure something out.

LUKE. You know, I just saw her, at the Tribal Complex, teaching her language class –

BOBBIE. You takin' it?

LUKE. Been going every week.

BOBBIE. That's great.

LUKE. I'm gonna quit.

BOBBIE. The language program?

LUKE. The bank.

BOBBIE. Oh. Why?

LUKE. I just, I've always worked there, you know, 'cause that's where my dad worked.

BOBBIE. You've done well.

LUKE. They gave me a promotion.

BOBBIE. You're smart.

LUKE. Not as smart as Jane.

BOBBIE. You're a different kinda smart.

LUKE. I can't do this. And I won't. If they wanna do this, they can find somebody else.

BOBBIE. And they will. They always have. But we need folks like you. To walk in both worlds.

For yer parents, and our parents, and our parents' parents – we only ever lost. You make a treaty. White man breaks the treaty. You cultivate the land. White man takes the land. You build a home. White man takes the home. But you, you got an education. No one can take that from you.

Just remember, you can talk their talk, walk their walk, but the moment you forget who you are, they have you. And then you're walkin' in one world, not two.

Alright tell me, what do you know? In Lenape?

LUKE. Oh, I uh –

BOBBIE. Come on now.

LUKE. *(Mispronounces it.)* Nkaski alenixsi (I can speak Lenape.)

BOBBIE. *(Is one hundred percent accurate, corrects **LUKE**.)* Nkaski alenixsi.

LUKE. I'm like not even close.

BOBBIE. You're very close. It just takes practice.

I knew your mom. Went to school together. And when we first met, when we were real little, Lenape was all she spoke.

LUKE. She never spoke to me.

BOBBIE. Sometimes as parents we think we're protecting our kids, shielding them from pain, but then we only hurt them.

Our language is who we are. I wish your mom was here to see you bring it back.

Twenty-Three

*(Manhattan. March 2008. **JANE** rushes into Dick's office, joining **DICK** and **JOE**.)*

JANE. We're down twenty-one percent. It's Bear.

*(**JANE** turns the TV on.)*

NEWSCAST. *(Voice-over.)* In the wake of Bear's collapse, Lehman Brothers is scrambling to reassure investors about the impact of the mortgage crisis on its own assets. Shares of the firm are under a great deal of pressure this morning. Dick Fuld, a thirty-nine-year veteran of Lehman and the longest running CEO of a major investment bank on Wall Street, has pulled the firm back from the brink during other crises. But today, for the first time, investors are questioning his leadership.

DICK. This is a shitshow.

*(**DICK** picks up his remote and clicks the TV off.)*

JANE. No one saw this one coming –

JOE. We're down twenty-one percent.

DICK. I just lost ninety million dollars, personally.

JANE. Our stock's evaporating.

DICK. What do our earnings look like?

JANE. They're top notch this quarter. We beat every prediction.

JOE. You see! It's the goddamn short sellers! Short and distort, that's their game.

JANE. We need to try for a capital raise.

DICK. We just made our shareholders money.

JANE. That's not what the market thinks.

JOE. We don't need capital.

JANE. Our stock is falling fast.

JOE. But our earnings are the best they've ever been.

JANE. Everyone's looking to us for a solution.

DICK. For a problem we didn't create.

JANE. This is about perception.

DICK. It's not like we pointed a gun at anyone's head and said "buy a home."

> (**SE-KET-TU-MAY-QUA** *enters and puts his arm on* **JANE.**)

SE-KET-TU-MAY-QUA. Here, let's sit for a moment.

Twenty-Four

(Manahatta.)

*(**DICK** and **JOE** exit and **JANE** joins* **SE-KET-TU-MAY-QUA**.*)*

LE-LE-WA'-YOU. We shouldn't be here.

SE-KET-TU-MAY-QUA. Yes, but I have something to give you.

*(**SE-KET-TU-MAY-QUA** pulls out the wampum necklace.)*

This was my mother's. She made it, from the shells she collected, here, along the shore. It's the only thing of hers I have left.

(The sun rises. He places the necklace around her neck.)

LE-LE-WA'-YOU. Promise me we will never leave.

SE-KET-TU-MAY-QUA. This is my home.

LE-LE-WA'-YOU. I want it to be the home of our children.

*(**JAKOB** enters, carrying a gun. He stops in his tracks and aims it directly at* **SE-KET-TU-MAY-QUA**. **LE-LE-WA'-YOU** *is the first to spot* **JAKOB** *and screams.)*

No!

*(**JAKOB** lowers his gun.)*

JAKOB. Le-le-wa'-you!

LE-LE-WA'-YOU. Don't shoot!

JAKOB. You can't be here.

SE-KET-TU-MAY-QUA. Yes, but –

JAKOB. I'm serious.

> *(He looks to make sure no one else is around, and then in a rather hushed tone:)*

Get out of here. Now! Before someone sees me talking to you and shoots all three of us!

VOICE FROM OFFSTAGE. Hey! You see any over that way?

JAKOB. No. No Indians here.

VOICE FROM OFFSTAGE. Let's head over to the Broad Way.

JAKOB. Alright!

VOICE FROM OFFSTAGE. We'll find Indians there.

JAKOB. *(In hushed tones.)* Get out of here. Now. And be careful. The Governor has promised ten fathoms of wampum to any colonist who brings him a redskin. *(Pronounced as one word, not two.)*

> **(JAKOB** *exits.)*

LE-LE-WA'-YOU. They're trading our skin for wampum.

Twenty-Five

(Manahatta. A few days later.)

*(***PETER MINUIT*** *sits at the desk with the tulip.* **JAKOB** *enters.)*

JAKOB. That's sixty more. Dead.

PETER MINUIT. How did this Indian manage to kill sixty of my men?

JAKOB. He used the guns that you gave him –

PETER MINUIT. I never *gave* him anything –

JAKOB. The guns you *traded* with him when we purchased the island.

PETER MINUIT. I want his flesh.

JAKOB. Black Beaver?

PETER MINUIT. I don't want to hear that you've killed him, I need to see it. You know where he lives?

JAKOB. None of the Lenape "live" in one place. They have hunting grounds and trading trails and –

PETER MINUIT. You know where to find him.

JAKOB. There's a place. I know where he goes.

PETER MINUIT. Good. And I need you to build a wall.

JAKOB. On your farm?

PETER MINUIT. On the island. To keep the rest of them out. You know, on the north side, where they usually come down to trade, along the Broad Way.

JAKOB. We don't have the resources to build a wall.

PETER MINUIT. It'll run east to west, starting at that street where they always dump their shells –

JAKOB. We have no capital.

PETER MINUIT. We have Negroes.

>*(**PETER MINUIT** stands up and pours himself and **JAKOB** a glass of brandy.)*

I know you like them. The Lenape. This is your home now, and you've formed an attachment. So I know. This is painful. But necessary. Sometimes we have to cut off a part to preserve the whole.

Finish Black Beaver, and I'll make you my Lieutenant Governor.

>*(**JANE** enters and speaks to **PETER MINUIT** and **JAKOB**.)*

JANE. We're down forty-eight percent.

Twenty-Six

(Manhattan. September 2008.)

(Dick's office.)

DICK. Short and distort, that's all they do.

JANE. We've got two banks that won't take our name.

JOE. Who?

JANE. HSBC and Deutsche.

DICK. Fuck HSBC.

JANE. We just lost 2.8 billion.

JOE. That's more than five dollars a share.

DICK. I just lost fifty million. Personally.

JANE. It's the house price index. It's not falling. It's plummeting.

JOE. I'm going to announce my resignation.

JANE. What?

DICK. Shut the fuck up and get me a cup of coffee.

JOE. People are upset, Dick. They're scared. Heads have to roll. If they don't, the firm stands to lose even more.

DICK. Sure, OK, someone has to go –

JOE. And it can't be you.

DICK. That's not your call.

JOE. So it has to be me.

DICK. *(Turns to* **JANE.***)* What do you think?

JANE. I don't think you should leave.

JOE. Not up to you, Snake.

DICK. *(Grabs the report out of* **JANE***'s hands.)* What's this?

JANE. Our quarterly earnings.

JOE. You wouldn't know this from reading the news right now, but we actually made our shareholders money this quarter.

DICK. How much?

JANE. Four hundred and eighty-nine million.

DICK. That's –

JANE. Eighty-one cents a share.

DICK. Great, we can announce this!

JOE. Yes.

DICK. And I want you to announce it.

JOE. I'm resigning.

DICK. Damnit Joe, the earnings call's in five minutes. You can't do that.

JOE. The world's not going to see it as good news unless they think something's about to change around here. And I mean really change.

DICK. We have liquidity.

JOE. They don't care about liquidity. They want to see change.

DICK. So if you don't announce our earnings who will?

JOE. Snake.

JANE. Me?

JOE. She can do it.

JANE. No I can't.

JOE. She's ready.

JANE. I'm not.

JOE. She'll signal change to the market.

DICK. She'll signal something, that's for sure. Alright, Joe.

(*To* **JANE**.) Congratulations, Snake. You've been promoted. Know what you need to say?

JANE. No. What do I say?

DICK. Whatever it takes to convince the world we're not the next Bear Stearns.

(**DICK** *hands the report back to* **JANE**.)

JOE. You're ready for this.

DICK. (*Checks his cell and sees the time.*) Shit, Snake, pick up the phone. WE'RE ON!

(**JANE** *picks up the phone from the desk.* **SE-KET-TU-MAY-QUA** *enters and approaches the rock.*)

JANE. Hello, and thank you for joining us for this call regarding the firm's quarterly financial results. My name is Jane Snake –

SE-KET-TU-MAY-QUA. (*Looking for her.*) Le-le-wa'-you?

JANE. I am the firm's new...

DICK. COO.

JANE. COO.

SE-KET-TU-MAY-QUA. Where are you?

JANE. It's clear that in the last few days, we've witnessed unprecedented volatility –

(**SE-KET-TU-MAY-QUA** *hears a noise that makes him suspicious they aren't alone at the rock.*)

(**SE-KET-TU-MAY-QUA** *makes an audible call.*)

JANE. Not only in our sector but also across the entire marketplace.

And so that's why we're making a few changes around here.

But first, let me make something very clear. The lies, the deception, the toxic RMBS collateral that destroyed Bear Stearns – you won't find that on our balance sheet. There's a reason Bear failed. They don't trade the same way we do.

So what's not clear is why so many in the market feel the need to act from a place of fear.

> (**JOE** *and* **DICK** *cheer* **JANE** *on while they watch their stock rise on their Bloomberg terminal.*)

JOE. Give it to 'em Snake!

JANE. A simple review of the numbers reveals that there's no cause for concern.

> *(Gunshot.)*

DICK. That's right.

JANE. Our quarterly earnings are at four hundred and eighty-nine million, or eighty-one cents a share.

JOE. You got this.

JANE. That's higher than any of the analyst forecasts and –

DICK. Our stock –

JANE. Is well-within the range of this firm's past earnings.

DICK. *(Points to Bloomberg terminal.)* It's climbing!

JANE. Although everyone in the market is busy screaming fire –

> *(Gunshots.)*

(The gunshots continue. **SE-KET-TU-MAY-QUA** *dances to secure his safety. His movement could be literal, or could be more akin to a dance.)*

(Note: the gunshots can vary and do not need to occur as frequently as they appear in the script so long as there is an intentional rhythm behind their placement.)

DICK. It's coming back!

JANE. The facts, the numbers themselves –

(Gunshot.)

Demonstrate that we have liquidity.

(Gunshot.)

This firm's efforts to reduce leverage and increase liquidity have paid off –

JOE. Still climbing!

(Gunshot.)

JANE. And our earnings show that.

DICK. We're blowing up!

(Gunshot.)

JANE. Thank you for joining us for today's quarterly earnings call. And as you can see –

DICK. Don't stop now!

JANE. There is nothing to fear.

(A loud gunshot. **SE-KET-TU-MAY-QUA** *falls.)*

JOE. YES!

DICK. Total success.

JOE. You did it Snake.

> (**JOE** *exits*.)

JANE. And on a final note, it is with great sadness that we have received the announcement of Joe Gregory's resignation. Although our firm has lost a fierce financial warrior, we look forward to our future and continue to take pride in our position as a financial pillar on Wall Street. As always, you know where to find us. Thank you.

> (**JANE** *hangs up the phone.*)

> (**JAKOB** *enters, knife in hand. He kneels next to* **SE-KET-TU-MAY-QUA**, *confirms that it is indeed* **SE-KET-TU-MAY-QUA**, *and then with his knife, cuts* **SE-KET-TU-MAY-QUA***'s flesh.*)

> (**JANE** *turns and sees* **SE-KET-TU-MAY-QUA** *dead, on the ground next to the rock.*)

LE-LE-WA'-YOU. No.

> (**JAKOB** *stands, flesh in hand, and sees* **LE-LE-WA'-YOU**. *They regard one another.*)

> (**JAKOB** *exits.* **LE-LE-WA'-YOU** *collapses by* **SE-KET-TU-MAY-QUA***'s side. She holds him.*)

> (*After a moment,* **TOOSH-KI-PA-KWIS-I** *enters, carrying her sister's baby. She goes to her* **SISTER***'s side.*)

TOOSH-KI-PA-KWIS-I. We have to go.

> (**LE-LE-WA'-YOU** *shakes her head no.*)

Sister, before they kill all of us.

> (**TOOSH-KI-PA-KWIS-I** *grabs her* **SISTER**, *forcing her to stand.*)

> (**JANE**'s *hands, and perhaps other parts of her body, are covered in blood.*)

DICK. Shit Snake, you nailed it!

JANE. I'm so thankful it's over.

DICK. Over? I wish you never hung up! As long as you were on that call, our stock kept climbing!

> (**DICK** *pulls out the bottle of brandy.* **LE-LE-WA'-YOU** *stares at her lover's lifeless body.*)

TOOSH-KI-PA-KWIS-I. You're a mother now. He'll understand.

> (**TOOSH-KI-PA-KWIS-I** *gestures for her* **SISTER** *to follow her, then exits.*)

DICK. You've had brandy?

JANE. I'm not sure that I have.

> (**DICK** *pours* **JANE** *and himself a drink.*)

DICK. Well you absolutely must give it a try. This bottle is a fine, or rather, a great, indeed I think the greatest, spirit ever made.

> (*They drink their brandy.* **JANE**'s *bloody hands leave blood on her glass and anything she touches.*)

This is all nonsense, if you ask me. Pure nonsense.

JANE. It's like derivative is a dirty word.

DICK. All of a sudden you can't say "derivative" or Wolf Blitzer has a heart attack.

JANE. Journalists just don't understand.

DICK. They're not mathematicians, like you.

JANE. Humans have been trading derivatives for centuries.

DICK. Exactly.

JANE. Like the Dutch. They traded derivatives in tulips.

DICK. Derivatives are like guns. The problem isn't the tools.

JANE. It's the people using them.

DICK. I doubted Joe.

JANE. I'm going to miss him.

DICK. I told him, what the hell Joe, you think you can hire someone with a degree in mathematics and expect them to sell securities?

JANE. Financial mathematics. I have a degree in –

(**DICK** *pours more brandy into Jane's glass.*)

DICK. You like this brandy?

JANE. It's different.

DICK. I knew you'd like it. Keep this up Snake, you're really going places.

JANE. You think so?

DICK. Are you kidding me? I traded bonds my whole career, I mean, until I joined management. And I never saw a woman trade mortgage bonds until '86. You know what makes this country so great?

(**JANE** *isn't sure.*)

People like you can start with nothing, work hard, and look where you end up? I mean, you don't see any Native Americans running investment banks in London, now do you?

JANE. No. I guess not.

(**DICK** *raises his glass for a toast.*)

DICK. To Manhattan!

JANE. To Manhattan!

Twenty-Seven

(Anadarko. Bobbie's house.)

*(**BOBBIE** enters carrying a bag of groceries. **DEBRA** is sitting at the desk, foreclosure notice in hand.)*

BOBBIE. Ya shoulda seen the line at the store. Took me twenty minutes just to get up to the register. And they were out of milk. Coulda drove to Chickasha to get some, but I think I'll just go tomorrow, gotta head that way anyways to visit your auntie... Deb? You alright?

DEBRA. You mortgaged the house?

*(**BOBBIE** nods.)*

Why?

BOBBIE. Needed the money.

DEBRA. There are lots of ways to get money that don't involve mortgaging our home.

BOBBIE. This was the best way.

DEBRA. How can you say that?

BOBBIE. The surgery cost sixty thousand.

DEBRA. But IHS –

BOBBIE. Wouldn't cover it.

DEBRA. OK. Fine. So we owe some money –

BOBBIE. I owe some money.

DEBRA. Maybe they can put you on a repayment plan, or adjust the monthly payments. There has to be something. Did you tell Jane?

BOBBIE. She wouldn't understand.

DEBRA. She won't if you don't tell her. Mom! You have to tell somebody!

BOBBIE. I'm tellin' you. Right now.

DEBRA. Auction's on Wednesday.

(**BOBBIE** *exits. She returns carrying a box.*)

BOBBIE. Will you help me pack?

DEBRA. No I will not help you pack.

(She sets the box down and begins to go through the contents, searching.)

BOBBIE. Started last night, after you went to bed. Guess that's the good thing about moving. Lived my whole life here, and I'm just now remembering what we have.

DEBRA. Mom.

BOBBIE. Found a hymnal last night, all these years, sittin' under Charlie's boots, in the closet. It's got hundreds of pages of hymns, translated in Lenape –

DEBRA. That's OK.

BOBBIE. It was your dad's.

DEBRA. Mom –

BOBBIE. Thought you could use it, ya know, for yer language program –

DEBRA. We stopped the language program.

BOBBIE. 'Cause you didn't get the grant? I thought Jane gave you lots of money –

DEBRA. Because we needed a speaker. To teach.

BOBBIE. You were teaching –

DEBRA. From a book. I can't speak Lenape.

BOBBIE. So you quit.

DEBRA. I didn't quit.

BOBBIE. Seems to me you did.

DEBRA. Me, what about you?

BOBBIE. I'm not the one refusin' a hymnal.

DEBRA. You told Dad you were gonna teach.

BOBBIE. He asked me –

DEBRA. And you said yes.

BOBBIE. I did.

DEBRA. And then he died and you quit.

BOBBIE. I couldn't do it –

DEBRA. You quit the language program. You quit me. But really, you wanna know why I'll never forgive you. You quit Dad.

(Beat.)

BOBBIE. I was a kid, about five or six, when the BIA showed up. Walked inside the front door, this front door, grabbed me outta my parents' arms, and took me away. To Riverside. Kept me there for eight years. Made me speak English. Always. Anyone caught speakin' Lenape got a beatin'.

That's where I met him. Your dad. One day, he decided to tell me how he felt. So when he thought no one was lookin', as we passed each other in the hallway, he said: *ktaholel.*

He didn't know the word for love in English.

Guess no one taught us that. One of the teachers, she overheard him. She grabbed his arm real hard, dragged him down the hall, and then she beat him. 'Til he was unconscious.

*(**DEBRA** goes to her **MOTHER**.)*

BOBBIE. My biggest regret is that I didn't speak Lenape with you girls. But back then, you learned not to speak. Every ounce of your being was spent just tryin' to blend in. Be somethin' you ain't. No matter how much Indian ya had in you, they did their best to whip it out.

The other day I woke up and I listened – and then I realized I don't hear it no more. Charlie's gone, and ain't no one speakin' it. That's 'cause I buried it. And now it's six feet under.

(**DEBRA** *embraces her* **MOTHER.**)

Twenty-Eight

(Manhattan, at Lehman Brothers.)

*(***JANE*** *sits in her office, watching TV.* **DICK** *enters.)*

NEWSCAST. *(Voice-over.)* Breaking news just coming in. Despite the move to nationalize Fannie and Freddie, the market is still in negative territory across the board. Investors are now focusing their attention on Lehman Brothers amid fresh reports that the Nation's fourth largest investment bank may be on the brink of bankruptcy.

*(***DICK*** *snaps off the TV.)*

JANE. We're at three dollars a share.

DICK. Tell me something I don't already know.

JANE. We need to sell the firm.

DICK. I'm not selling my firm for three dollars –

JANE. We're at three dollars.

DICK. Do you know where we were one year ago? Eighty-seven. Eighty-seven dollars a share!

JANE. Now we're at three. And we lost Barclay's.

DICK. I thought you said we had them.

JANE. We did.

DICK. What the hell happened?

JANE. Their regulator. He won't approve the deal.

DICK. What'd he say?

JANE. They refuse to import any more of our American cancer.

DICK. Fucking British. And now Ken Lewis won't return my calls.

JANE. They're buying Merrill.

DICK. Merrill?! Did the Government just fuck with my deal?

JANE. They're signing the papers now.

DICK. So no one wants to buy Lehman.

JANE. No one.

DICK. Call Paulson.

(**DICK** *exits.*)

Twenty-Nine

(Anadarko. September 2008. Before the auction.)

*(**DEBRA** and **BOBBIE** are packing. **JANE** enters.)*

JANE. What the hell is going on here?

DEBRA. Nice to see you Jane.

JANE. I have seven voicemails, all from Luke, telling me my family is in crisis. I tried to call but no one answered. I called for five days. Straight. No answer.

DEBRA. Phone's been disconnected.

JANE. Yeah. I noticed. Did it occur to you that perhaps you should reconnect it?

DEBRA. We can't –

JANE. Or you won't? I had to get on a plane, two planes because there're no direct flights to Lawton, and bring myself out here to see if you're still alive.

DEBRA. Thanks for coming.

JANE. Have you even turned on the news? Everything I've worked for is gone. Everything I built, it's been destroyed. No one's lending, they can't. That means there's no capital, no liquidity.

And I know you don't care, but you should. Yes, our capital allowed a lot of idiots to take out loans they never could repay, but without that capital, our entire economy stops running.

*(Beat. **BOBBIE** exits. **JANE** looks to **DEBRA**.)*

DEBRA. We're losing our home.

JANE. What?

DEBRA. Mom mortgaged the house.

JANE. What?

DEBRA. She took out a loan –

JANE. You didn't tell me.

DEBRA. I didn't know.

JANE. Why?

DEBRA. She had to pay for Dad's surgery.

JANE. His surgery?

DEBRA. IHS wouldn't pay.

JANE. You should have asked me –

DEBRA. I didn't know.

JANE. You live here!

DEBRA. Not anymore. Auction's on Wednesday.

(**DEBRA** *hands* **JANE** *the notice.* **JANE** *reads it.*)

JANE. We're going to lose our home.

DEBRA. Mom and I, we're losing our home. You're losing a memory. Of something you never understood.

(**MICHAEL** *and* **LUKE** *enter.*)

MICHAEL. Looks great. Thanks for cleaning up.

(*He looks at* **LUKE**.)

I told him not to call her.

DEBRA. It's alright.

LUKE. She deserved to know.

DEBRA. Better you than me. She never listens to me.

JANE. I'm standing right here.

DEBRA. These are all the keys, front and back door. Oh, and the garage.

(**DEBRA** *hands* **MICHAEL** *the keys.*)

MICHAEL. I'm sure we could negotiate a few more days if you need it –

DEBRA. Don't sweat it.

MICHAEL. I hate kicking you guys out like this.

DEBRA. We're packed and ready to go.

MICHAEL. You know the church has programs for folks who lose their homes.

DEBRA. We'll be fine.

MICHAEL. You clear the garage?

DEBRA. Let me show you what's left.

(**DEBRA** *and* **MICHAEL** *exit.* **JANE** *turns to* **LUKE**.)

JANE. You made this loan?

LUKE. She told me not to tell you.

JANE. *(Waiving the auction notice.)* And you told her to take out an ARM?

LUKE. I thought it was a bad idea, but –

JANE. You made it. You originated the loan.

LUKE. I did. And then I told my dad not to let you securitize it.

JANE. What?

LUKE. The bank, we sell all of our adjustable rate mortgages to a Lehman holding company. What are you again? Executive Vice President of Capital Markets? What do you oversee, securitizations?

LUKE. Dad and I convinced the bank to keep your mom's loan on our balance sheet. Something we almost never do. But we did this time because I knew. You wouldn't be able to live with yourself if your mom's home became the collateral guaranteeing a tranche in one of your precious CDOs.

> (**DEBRA** *and* **MICHAEL** *return, mid-discussion.*)

MICHAEL. It's no problem. We can remove all that.

> (**JANE** *turns to* **MICHAEL**.)

JANE. How much?

> (*Beat.*)

How much is due on the mortgage?

MICHAEL. Legally, I cannot divulge that sort of confidential information to anyone but the debtor, at least not without –

JANE. Just tell me how much my mom owes.

LUKE. Forty-seven thousand, five hundred, and sixty-five dollars.

> (**JANE** *digs in her purse and pulls out her checkbook. She writes a check. She hands it to* **MICHAEL**.)

> (**BOBBIE** *enters, carrying her wampum necklace. She turns to* **DEBRA**.)

BOBBIE. Need to put this somewhere safe.

MICHAEL. Good news, Bobbie! (*Holds out the check.*) Jane paid off your mortgage.

BOBBIE. No.

JANE. Mom.

BOBBIE. I'm not letting her buy it.

MICHAEL. Well technically you can't stop her –

BOBBIE. I said no.

JANE. If I don't buy it, someone else will.

BOBBIE. Probably, yeah.

JANE. You would rather some stranger buy your house than your own daughter?

BOBBIE. Yes.

JANE. It's fine, Mom. I can afford it.

BOBBIE. With what? The money you made from all those other idiots who got loans they can't repay?

(Beat.)

JANE. I shouldn't have said that. I'm sorry. I didn't know. You didn't tell me. How am I supposed to know if you don't tell me? And Mom, this is crazy. You don't need to leave. You can stay. Please, just let me buy your home.

*(**BOBBIE** takes the check from **MICHAEL**'s hand and rips it into several pieces.)*

BOBBIE. Some things are not for sale.

JANE. So you'll be homeless?

BOBBIE. We're Lenape. We're never homeless.

JANE. Losing your home is the definition of homeless.

*(**BOBBIE** holds out the necklace in her hands.)*

BOBBIE. This is real wampum, from the shores of Manahatta. Someone in our family carried this necklace the whole way down our Trail of Broken Treaties.

From Manahatta to Pennsylvania, my great-great-great-great grandma carried this necklace. From

Pennsylvania to Ohio. And Ohio to Missouri. Missouri to Texas. And when we were forced to leave the Brazos Reserve and move here, my grandma carried this necklace the whole way. She gave it to my mom. And my mom gave it to me.

We don't own anything. We live in our home because the Creator gave it to us. So they can try. But they can never take our home.

Every time they make us leave, we carry our home with us.

> (**BOBBIE** *puts the wampum necklace on* **JANE**. **BOBBIE** *picks up her final box and exits the home.)*

> (**MICHAEL** *and* **LUKE** *each pick up their final load and follow* **BOBBIE** *out.)*

> (**JANE** *stumbles out the door and lands in Charlie's chair on the porch.* **DEBRA** *makes one last round, picks up the final box, and exits onto the porch, where she finds her* **SISTER***, collapsed in Charlie's chair.)*

> (**DEBRA** *hands* **JANE** *her purse.)*

DEBRA. You headed back?

> (**JANE** *does not respond.)*

I know it's a long trip, but I'm glad you made –

JANE. Dad used to sit out here and sing. Late into the night. I'd open my window. He didn't know, but I always stayed up and listened.

I was jealous. Dad taught you to sing, but he never, I think he always knew. I'd be the one to leave. And never come home.

DEBRA. He asked where you were. Just before the surgery. He wasn't really coherent, I think he forgot. So I told him, I said Daddy, she's at her interview. Remember she flew up there and she's gonna interview, and if she gets it, if she gets this job, she's gonna live in Manhattan.

He just smiled and said… "Machi. Machi Manahatta."

JANE. I don't know what that means.

DEBRA. Go home. Go home to Manahatta.

Thirty

(Manhattan. September 15, 2008. The next morning. Lehman Brothers.)

*(**DICK** sits at his desk as **JANE** enters, wearing the necklace of wampum. The sun starts to rise over the East River. The first beams of light break into Dick's office.)*

JANE. I know I'm late, I'm sorry, family crisis back at home. What'd I miss?

DICK. The collapse of our entire economy.

JANE. Did you call Goldman?

DICK. I couldn't. I was stuck in a six hour board meeting.

JANE. I'll call Goldman.

DICK. It's too late.

JANE. They could extend a line of credit.

DICK. Paulson says the markets will be in a panic if this isn't resolved by the time they open.

JANE. So what does he suggest?

DICK. Bankruptcy.

JANE. We have some liquidity problems –

DICK. We have no liquidity.

JANE. Maybe the government –

DICK. This isn't AIG. We don't get a sweetheart deal.

JANE. Don't you think –

DICK. We have no choice.

JANE. You think we have to declare bankruptcy.

DICK. I already did.

(They stand in silence.)

Snake, you can do just about anything you want. Me, I'm toast. Finished. Probably facing a billion lawsuits. But you, you're gonna be recruited. Headhunters are gonna call. Goldman. J.P. Morgan. They'll all want you. Unless you decide to call it quits, you know, go back home.

JANE. Home?

DICK. To Oklahoma.

JANE. This. This is my home. I didn't understand at first. Didn't remember. But now, watching the sun rise over the East River. I see it.

DICK. See what?

JANE. What my ancestors saw.

(**TOOSH-KI-PA-KWIS-I** *and* **MOTHER** *enter.* **MOTHER** *carries Le-Le-Wa'-You's baby girl.)*

This island. Manahatta. Our home.

The Dutch built a wall on Wall Street to keep us out. To make us leave our home.

But I came back. I came home. And I climbed all the way to the top.

They're saying millions of Americans will lose their homes. Because of this. Because of us.

I studied math because I love patterns. They're reliable. Predictable. But what if we need to break them? Can we?

(Her fingers run over the wampum necklace around her neck.)

I'd like to at least try.

(She looks back out over the East River.)

Machi. Machi Manahatta.

The End

www.ingramcontent.com/pod-product-compliance
Lightning Source LLC
Chambersburg PA
CBHW070330120726

47909CB00008B/2670